SECOND GOAL

Stephanie Orfali

AND/OR PRESS
1976 BERKELEY, CALIFORNIA

AND/OR PRESS
P.O. Box 2246
Berkeley, CA 94702

ISBN: 0-915904-11-X

photos by Hans Hetzel & members of the family

layout by Bonnie Smetts

THE CHARACTERS OF THE STORY

The family and their friends:

Willy, the owner of the bar, also employed by the São Paulo Light and Power Company as contract supervisor

Donna Anna Maria or *Annemarie,* the reluctant worker in the bar, the narrator of the story

Wolfi, their 14 year old son, a worldwise young man

Angela, their 12 year old daughter, an excellent cook and housekeeper

Enrico, their 8 year old son, who has trouble making friends

The Bambino, the baby of the family, 4 years old

The Müller Family, newly arrived from Germany

Kurt, Willy's assistant, friend of the family, and an ardent amateur photographer

Francisco, Willy's cousin, the family's only relative in São Paulo

Aurora, the maid whose story will be found in the appendix

The patrons of the bar and their families:

Jussuf, a dashing young Lebanese peddler

Mylorde, a venerable old man, the philosopher and sage of the neighborhood

Donna Esmeralda, his wife, considered a saint by her friends and neighbors

Carmen, their pretty little foster daughter

Sezinho, a sharp little boy, protege of the Professora

Donna Maria, his mother, a mulatto

Apparecida, his lazy, but pretty sister

Senhor Alberto, Apparecida's weekend boy friend

A little blond mulatto baby, their child

Senhor Abraham, a rich Jewish landlord, owner of a shoe store and card bearing member of the Communist party of Brazil

Donna Rachel, his wife and caretaker of the houses

Danny, their son, friend of Wolfi, and admirer of Angela

Senhor Moses, Senhor Abraham's brother, owner of the furniture store

Senhor Carlos, the watchmaker, a widower

Rosa, his pretty daughter

Senhor Ernesto, landlord of the bar, a miser; the story of his family is in the appendix

Donna Anna, his wife, an excellent cook

João, their fat son who shows no interest in girls

Toninho, the Japanese greengrocer, whose story is in the appendix

Donna Rita, his wife

Walther, his son, Enrico's friend

Eight little Japanese boys, Toninho's other children

Senhor Nair, a disk jockey with a sexy voice

Donna Irma, his barren wife

Chico and Emilio, two gay bachelors

Donna Linda, the Professora, teacher and alcoholic

Roberta, the whore

Nelson, a fat boy, and bully of the neighborhood, Enrico's enemy

The law:

Captain Alfredo from the homicide division of the São Paulo Police Department

A number of unidentified police men, and fingerprint experts

INTRODUCTION

This is the story of one of the most difficult weeks of my life.

It happened in a suburb of São Paulo, Brazil, in the late fifties. We left Brazil in 1957 to live in the U.S.A.

Since English is not my native language, and since I had to translate all of the dialog from either German or Portuguese into English, I am aware that my story is not written in perfect English. The reader has to forgive me my German accent.

I have changed the names of persons and places, and the basic plot of the story is fiction. The locale is quite authentic. Additional information about life in Brazil will be found in the appendix.

The Bar with Annemarie and the children.

Chapter One

SUNDAY MORNING, JUNE 20

Sunrays filtered through the partly open louvers and played on the wallpaper and the bed spreads. Tiny dots of dust danced gayly in the bright bands of light. Birds sang in the dew fresh garden, and hummingbirds hovered above the brightly colored flowers.

Suddenly, a thunderbolt wrecked the friendly scene.

I woke up and turned the alarm clock off. Sun, garden, flowers, birds disappeared. It was cold and pitchdark on this June morning in Sao Paulo, Brazil, in the Southern Hemisphere.

I slipped silently out of the bed into the hostile world without turning on the light. I did not want to wake Willy, my peacefully sleeping husband, who earned his few hours of Sunday morning sleep by hard work during the week. I cursed the cold and the darkness under my breath and went to the even colder bathroom. There I turned on the light, dressed quickly, and washed my hands and face. I cautiously brushed my teeth, carefully warming up the water in my mouth to soften the pain in my decayed teeth.

Running hot water was a luxury that we could not afford. We had only an electric shower that supplied a modest stream of tepid water. Right now it was far too cold for a shower; maybe I would take one at noon.

I felt too sorry for myself to put on any makeup. The dishes from yesterday's supper were still stacked up unwashed in the kitchen sink, but there was no time now to wash them. I tiptoed to the children's room and tried to wake up Wolfi, our eldest boy. At first he did not react at all. Then he grunted something and turned around in his bed. I shook him again, and he finally woke up.

"I'll get up in a minute," he said and turned his back to me.

I hoped for the best and left the house. Panthera Negra, the black cat, also known by the name of Trige, waited in front of the door. She rubbed herself against my legs and then stretched herself, telling me good morning. Panthera entered the house only on special occasions; her realm was our bar where she fulfilled her duties with great aplomb. She had two chores: first she had to give the bar a friendly, homey atmosphere which she accomplished by draping herself attractively on one of the chairs and purring melodiously; the second task was to keep the bar reasonably free of mice.

Between Panthera and me existed a love-hate relationship. Normally I was nice to her, gave her milk, petted her between the ears, and let her sit in my ample warm lap, but when I was drunk, I could be very cruel to her.

I remember with shame the time I picked her up by the tail, whirled her three times around my head, and let go. The cat sailed through the air, and I watched fascinated as she landed finally on her four paws and scampered away.

Today I greeted her politely, said, "Good morning, Trige," and started on my way, followed by Panthera. The Rua Promirim where we lived ran parallel to the Avenida Alta Vista where we owned a bar. I had to climb the steep Rua Bonita to get there. It was nearly seven o'clock, high time to prepare everything for the Sunday morning business. But, as unfortunately too often, the door was jammed, and I could not open the shutters.

'What can I do?' I asked myself. 'Should I go back and get Wolfi, or should I wait for a passer-by to help me?'

Before I could decide, I saw that Jussuf's station wagon was parked in the avenida. He got out and opened the door for me. He was very angry.

"Donna Anna Maria," he said, "this is already the third time that I pass from here. Don't you remember that I have to put up my booth before seven thirty when the avenida will be closed for traffic?"

I knew that the avenida would be closed, but I had forgotten that Jussuf had put the boards for his booth in the weekly market in our store room because he was in the process of moving to another suburb of São Paulo.

Jussuf stood six feet two in his stockinged feet. He was a splendid specimen of virile manhood. His hair and his mustache were raven black and as shiny as freshly polished shoes. His mouth was red, large and sensuous, his nose was bold and slightly beaked. Only his eyes were beady and shifty and had a vague, empty look. However, this was not always noticed because his eyes were usually narrowed down to a slit behind his engaging grin that could melt a glacier. In short, he was one of the most eligible bachelors of Vila Alta Vista. His fiancee was a pretty girl from a well-to-do family, but rumors had it that they had a fight last week. I assumed that the row was the reason why Jussuf was moving to another suburb.

A peddler with his backpack or a mule is an important fixture in every thinly populated area of this world. Jussuf was a modern version of the eternal peddler. His station wagon was his transportation and shop. Every Monday he drove into the villages, hamlets and scattered farms in the interior of the state of São Paulo where maidens of all ages waited to hear the gossip from the capital and to buy his goods. He sold cosmetics, ribbons, sewing utensils, knick-knacks and cheap jewelry. Fridays, he returned to São Paulo to replenish his stock, see the girls at home, and to open his booth on Sunday in the market of Alta Vista and afterwards get soundly drunk and sleep the rest of the day.

We entered the bar, Jussuf put his boards in his wagon and then returned to the bar.

"I want to give you my new address. Give me a *cafezinho* while I draw a plan."

"The coffee is not yet ready, and I don't know why I need your address."

"You can never know, Donna Anna Maria. Maybe you will make me happy one day by being my guest," he said, handing me a paper with his address in Vila Paulina and a sketch of the streets.

"Don't get any notions, Jussuf. I am an old-fashioned married woman," I said with a little regret in my voice, as I put the paper in the bottom of the cash drawer under the bills and receipts.

Panthera was already inside the bar before we opened the shutters. I gave her a saucer full of milk and wondered how she got in and out of the bar while it was closed. I made a mental note that I should look in the store room to see whether it had a hole in the wall. At the moment I had no time for this; I had urgent work to do.

The avenida outside the bar was in a state of confusion because the merchants put up their stalls for the weekly market, the feira, in great haste and with all the verbose excitement of Latin America.

The *feira* stretched for about a mile throughout the avenida. Our bar was approximately in the middle. The stalls were on the sidewalks while the buyers walked in the street which was closed for traffic from seven-thirty in the morning to twelve-thirty in the afternoon. Jussuf's booth was not far from the bar.

I didn't mop up on Sunday mornings because the customers brought dirt in and littered like mad. I swept quickly, turned on the coffee urn and made fresh coffee with sugar. This sweet brew is sold in tiny cups for one cruzeiro under the name of *cafezinho,* but for breakfast we also sold coffee with milk in larger cups for five cruzeiros.

I then carried the heavy box with the bottled milk that stood in the street into the bar and stored the bottles in the refrigerator. The bag with bread, buns and sweet rolls was also put in the street in front of the door by the baker's boy, early in the morning, and had to be taken in.

Jussuf had opened only one of the two shutters. I did not open the shutter to the Rua Bonita because it was cold and windy. A gray morning dawned outside, but it was still dark in the bar, and I had to turn the lights on.

The sink was overflowing dirty dishes that I had to wash with cold water. Then I prepared little tidbits of sausage, cheese, olives, little pickles on toothpicks, and little open-faced sandwiches to be eaten between drinks. The electric griddle was dirty and I had to scrub it.

'Where the hell is Wolfi?' I asked myself. I needed his help because somebody had to start the ice cream maker. We made our own ice cream which gave us more profit than the ready-made ice cream that the neighbors sold, and the children of the area preferred our brand. I had invented my own interesting recipes, and while I was weighing the ingredients, a group of shivering merchants entered the bar.

"Is the coffee ready, Donna Anna Maria?"

"It will be ready in a minute, and I have some warm buns and sweet rolls."

"Five cafezinhos and five sweet rolls, please."

"And a pack of Camels."

"Two packs of Fiestas."

"One pinga."

I gave them the cigarettes from the shelf and poured the *pinga*, a shot of cheap rum from sugar cane of Brazil. I was tempted to pour a shot of it for myself too, but thought better of it. In the meantime the coffee was ready, and I filled a cup of it for myself after I had served the customers.

'Will I ever find time to make the damned ice cream?' I asked myself as I got busy with more customers. The ice cream needed two hours and had to be ready when the children came back from church.

I was glad when Sezinho came by to get milk, bread and butter for his family. The little mulatto boy with his tattered shirt and bare feet was small for his nine years, but he had elegant features and a friendly smile under his mop of kinky hair. He was my good friend and helper, for good money, of course.

"Sezinho, be an angel," I said pleadingly. "Go home, and wake up Wolfi. But be careful not to wake up Senhor Wilhelmo. Go from the back, and knock at the window in the boys' room. Tell Wolfi that I need him urgently."

The sink was again full of dirty dishes when Wolfi finally showed up.

"Good morning, Wolfi, please help me before you sit down for breakfast."

"Shit," said Wolfi instead of "good morning," but I was in no mood to start an argument about his use of language, especially since he slipped behind the counter and began to wash the dishes without further ado.

The ice cream was finally in the machine, and I had served a number of children who came in for bread, butter, and milk when Wolfi and I finally sat down for breakfast.

I wanted to discuss with Wolfi a matter that had caused me a nearly sleepless night. The evening before we had left Wolfi alone in charge of the bar because we took a test drive in a car that had been offered to us as a down payment for the bar which we wanted to sell.

When we returned to the bar Wolfi was sitting on a chair near the rear of the bar with the girl Roberta on his lap. Roberta seemed to be trying to kiss him while Wolfi was wriggling away from her.

Without any introduction I told Wolfi, "You know damn well how I feel about Roberta. What's the idea of horsing around with her?"

"Mama, please don't get excited. You know how she acts when she is drunk."

"Yes, I do know, and that is why I am worried. You are much too young to have anything to do with her."

"But Mama, she was completely plastered; she didn't know who she was, who I was, or where she was. I tried to get rid of her; I can't stand the dirty bitch."

"Was she alone with you in the bar?"

"What do you mean, alone? Both doors were open, and customers came and went. Roberta uses the bar as headquarters. She does this also when Papa is in the bar. She walks the avenida, and when she finds a customer they usually have a drink before they go over to her place. When they are done, they come sometimes in for another drink before Roberta stalks another victim in the avenida."

Wolfi explained Roberta's business methods in further detail with great pleasure as if he were an old man who tries to enlighten a child.

"I am so afraid she will seduce you one of these days."

"You should have more confidence in me. After all, it's you who has brought me up and taught me about right and wrong. And you know damn well that I would not leave the bar to go over to her place. Forget about it, and tell me what you accomplished."

"Another wild goose chase. The car is so old and weak it's only held together by rust and spittle. The tires are down to the thread, and the transmission needs a repair."

"Damn it, can't we ever get rid of this goddam bar? Senhor Nair told me that Papa had a lot of offers but he always comes up with one reason or the other why he can't sell."

I was sick and tired of this bar and had been eager for a long time to get rid of it. It ruined our family life and my health, and it had a corrupting influence on our four children. On the other hand this bar was our only possession. All our savings and the work of many tiring hours were invested in it.

"I wish we could get rid of it, Wolfi, but you must understand that we cannot give it away; we must get something worthwhile out of it for all our work and sacrifices."

Wolfi sighed. He went to serve customers who had entered the bar, while I went to the storeroom to get the beer and soft drinks that had to be put in the refrigerator. It was a dull, routine job and I had time to think.

About a year ago, Willy had a good job, and I made some money teaching French and German to individuals and small groups. This left me enough free time for the children, and we made many excursions to the city and suburbs of São Paulo. We had a great number of friends and lived a happy, rich life. When I remember those first years in Brazil, they seemed to be like a paradise. They were carefree years in spite of financial hardships. The trouble really began when our finances improved, and we had money left over, after all the expenses were paid. The problem was, what to do with the surplus money. We finally decided to buy a plot of land, a *terreno*, with the hope to build our own house on it later. We spent many happy Sunday afternoons visiting one or another of the many new subdivisions that were advertised in the outlying suburbs of São Paulo. We had not yet made up our minds where to buy, when friends of Willy's family arrived out of the blue sky with greetings and gifts from the Old Country.

The week before the Müllers dropped in so unexpectedly, a bar was offered to Willy for sale. The location was ideal—only one block from the house where we lived—but in the middle of the business center of Vila Alta Vista. Willy mentioned the offer to his friend, because Herr Müller had told him that he wanted to go into business and that he had some money to invest in it. Willy introduced Müller to the owner of the bar and they spent the Sunday morning there and were deeply impressed by the amount of business. Herr Müller wanted to buy the place right away; the only drawback was that he could not speak a word of Portuguese.

They returned home with glowing eagerness and asked us women to go with them and see for ourselves. When Frau Müller saw the bar, she went overboard with enthusiasm, picturing herself as "bardame" in a most respectable place.

The Müllers bought the bar two days later without further inquiries. Not only did they buy the bar, but they convinced Willy to go into business with them because they needed a partner who could speak the language.

The previous owner stayed for one day to introduce us to the clientele, and to show us the intricacies of the ice cream machine.

Then he took his money and left. We never saw him again.

Herr Müller and Willy worked out a schedule of labor and the division of profits. Willy kept his job at the São Paulo Light and Power Company, but he would help in the evening and on weekends. The Müllers would stay all day long in the bar and do the work, but until they had learned to speak Portuguese, either Wolfi or I would stay with them.

The first week was great. I felt more like a hostess than a business woman and enjoyed the company of so many people who were all friendly and polite. Our customers were a mixed lot of all colors and nationalities and from all walks of life. After all the fuss about racial superiority in Germany, it was pure joy to see people of all backgrounds mingle freely and interact socially without being pigeon-holed into stereotyped labels or origin.

But right from the beginning there was a snag. The four Müller children were not yet in school and played all day long in the bar. They took to taking sweets and ice cream without asking permission to do so. I kept my mouth shut for several days in the hope they would get sick from all that sweet stuff. Instead, they increased their rations.

The Müllers made no effort to enroll them in school. Frau Müller said that they should learn the language first, but did not arrange for lessons.

At last, I could stand it no longer and said that she should stop her children from eating all the time because we were losing too much of our profit. She got very angry and shouted:

"My children are no thieves, you have no business telling me what to do. This is my bar, and they can do as they wish."

I said no more because I did not want any friction. The next day while Herr Müller had his afternoon nap, we two women were alone in the bar while all the children were playing at our house.

"Please clean out the refrigerator and stock it with beer," said Frau Müller in an authoritative, matter-of-fact voice, as if I was her employee.

I got angry. "You have no business to order me around as if I was your servant," I shouted, "I own this place as much as you do."

"Shut up," she shouted back. "We are the owners. We have much more money invested than you."

"You couldn't do a damn thing without us. You don't know a word of Portuguese, and your runny-nosed children spoil all the business."

"And you make eyes at the men as if you were a whore."

This was as much as I could take. When Willy came home from work that evening, I told him what had happened. He was quite taken aback. He talked to Herr Müller, who also insisted that it was his bar, not ours, since he had four times as much money in it as we. He also said that he had talked to other Germans and that he wanted to move to the suburb of Brooklin, São Paulo, where most of the Germans lived, and where his children could go to a German school. He could even own a bar there without speaking Portuguese.

He said also that he did not like to serve negroes, Indians, and Japanese, and especially he did not like the idea that his wife was considered by such people as their equals, and had to serve them who were really her inferiors, and a pretty sorry lot. Willy could buy him out anytime and keep the place for himself.

Willy told him to go to hell. He was sick and tired to have the dirty Müller brats always underfoot, and he could have his money anytime.

We took a loan, bought Herr Müller out, and became the sole owners of the bar until we were able to sell it with a profit. From then on, I worked ten to eleven hours daily in the bar, seven days a week.

When people in Europe or America think of a bar, they usually think of a night club with girls and sex-oriented entertainment. A dark place where you can spend a lot of money. A Brazilian bar has none of the above features. It is a white-tiled, open place that sells coffee and alcoholic drinks, as well as soft drinks, and, as often as not, candies, ice cream and cigarettes.

Our bar was 25 feet long and 15 feet wide. We had also a store room for the bottled drinks which were delivered once a week. Panthera found a lively population of rats and mice when we moved in, but had by now gotten it under control. We also had a restroom which was very shabby despite my endeavors to keep it clean. Many tiles were broken, the mirror was blind, and the sink was cracked; the seat was loose, but we always postponed a repair for the time we would have a surplus. Until the time of this story, every penny of profit went to pay the initial loan.

The bar had corrugated iron shutters that opened to the north and east, but neither doors nor windows. The north entrance opened to the Avenida Alta Vista, and the east entrance to the Rua Bonita. On both sides of the Avenida were shops with residential dwellings in the upper stories. The bank was right across the street, next to a dental clinic. The bus coming from the city stopped in front of our bar, the bus to the city in front of the bank. Church and schools were just a few blocks away, and besides, we had the Sunday feira right in front of us.

The bar, which was a one-story building, as well as the little one-family house in which we lived, belonged to Senhor Ernesto, a rich Portuguese who was known throughout the neighborhood as a skinflint. The equipment of the bar and the stock of merchandise belonged to us, or rather, the holder of our mortgage.

The refrigerator with the ice cream machine stood right behind the east entrance. It was quite large, because it cooled not only the beer and soft drinks but also milk and butter which we sold to local families. A showcase for candy and a soft drink dispenser were near the entrance, so that the children did not have to enter the bar but made their purchases from the street. Nevertheless, children were always in the bar in close proximity to people that we, in other countries, would label undesirables.

The huge counter stood across the bar and was at least 18 feet long. It had a marble top. On it stood the shiny coffee urn, and a display case for refreshments. The rest of the counter top was empty to hold the cups and glasses of the customers who stood in front of the counter. The patrons drank their coffee or liquor while standing up, and talking with each other. The ever-changing combination of customers, friends and strangers, in earnest or bantering conversations is the basic charm of a Brazilian bar. The astonishing integration of people of many races and nationalities was a never-ending source of wonder to us.

Behind the counter were the sink, the griddle, the scale, and a small working area. Under the counter we stacked full and empty bottles. Our two small boys liked to stack the bottles while pinching or tickling the person working behind the counter.

The western wall had shelves up to the ceiling for wine, hard liquor, cigarettes, and the radio. A few bars already had TV sets, but ours was a lower middle class bar, and we could not afford one.

We had only three small, marble topped tables with chairs. Few customers sat down, except on Sundays, when we served food. The tables were mostly used by us because we took most of our meals right in the bar. My own social life took place sitting around these tables instead of a coffee table at home. I had many a Kaffeklatsch with an assortment of dear ladies from all walks of life, and a lot of gossip was created, enlarged upon and disseminated from here. The children did most of their homework in the bar. Whenever I had time, I used to look their homework over, study with them, and read their books in a desperate effort to further my own education about Brazil.

The floor was covered with tiles too worn out to get completely clean. My maid, Aurora, used to scrub them—without much success— just because it is expected from a good housewife. The lower part of the walls was covered with white, shiny ceramic tiles; the upper part was whitewashed, and covered with posters, mostly advertisements, but also beautiful photos of São Paulo by our friend Kurt, Willy's assistant at work and an ardent amateur photographer.

We never felt close enough to the bar to give it a name. It was commonly known as Senhor Willy's bar. Another bar, known as "A Preferida," was in the same building, but our customers preferred neither of the two. Instead they divided their business faithfully between the two of us. We had, however, the advantage of the corner and the ice cream machine.

We had a lot of traffic in the bar. It was rarely empty, and certainly looked as though it were pretty lucrative. But our expenses for rent, taxes, replenishing of the stock, interest on the loan, repayment, thefts, repairs, etc., were high. Our living expenses were paid from Willy's pay check. Our profit from the bar was used to pay our debt.

I was nearly finished with the preparations for the Sunday rush when Willy and the children showed up.

"I'm hungry," said Enrico without any greeting.

"I too," said the bambino.

Willy also dispensed with formalities, and said, "Let me finish with the bottles and prepare something to eat for us."

I made bacon and eggs for breakfast, and we all sat down to eat except Angela. She planned to go to communion and was fasting. So she took care of the customers while we ate. Afterwards, Willy took the children to mass.

Wolfi and I stayed in the bar and by the time the rest of the family returned, we were hard at work serving breakfast to the customers of the feira. Only one of our regular patrons was in the bar. Mylorde sat on a chair near the north entrance. He regarded the hustle and bustle in the avenida with his customary philosophical aloofness.

I never learned Mylorde's real name. Actually, I knew only a few of the family names of our customers. People were addressed by their first names or nicknames, with the title added depending upon familiarity. I was Donna Anna Maria to everyone, but Willy had a few friends who called him Willy instead of Senhor Willy or Senhor Guilhermo. Since some names are very common, diminutive forms of a name were often used like Toninho for Antonio, or Sezinho for Jose; sometimes epithets were used. Senhor Carlos was known as O Relogiero—the watchmaker—and the lady of our neighboring bar as A Calzuda, the one who wears the pants. Sometimes the nationality of a person was added to his name. Our friend Jussuf was commonly known as Jussuf, Filho de Sirio, and Roberta, the girl I resented so much, proudly called herself Roberta a Portuguesa because of her Portuguese father.

If you did not know the name of a person, you could always call him Patricio, compatriot, or Patrinio, godfather; you could call a lady Patricia or Madrinha.

Mylorde was an old, venerable man with deep furrows in his face which gave him the look of great wisdom. He had sparse grey hair, and was always clean shaven. His ears stood out from his head like the handles of a cup, and he had small deepset eyes, a prominent nose, and a small wrinkled mouth.

He was always formally dressed in a white shirt, tie and jacket, even during the worst heat. His suit was always freshly ironed, his shirts washed and starched and his tie never stained. His elegant appearance had probably won him his aristocratic nickname. Everyone treated him with reverence, and his advice was highly valued. He patronized all the bars in the avenida, but his favorite place was the chair at the entrance to our bar.

Mylorde lived with his statuesque wife, Donna Esmeralda, in one of the stateliest houses in Vila Alta Vista, right next to the church. They had no children of their own, but Donna Esmeralda raised foster children, one after the other, never more than one at a time. She treated the children as if they were her own, and never took money from their parents. When they were grown up, they always came back to Donna Esmeralda. She was a happy and doting grandmother to the children of her first three foster children.

At this time Donna Esmeralda was raising a pretty negro girl of about five years. Little Carmen wore snow white dresses and looked like a doll in a cartoon with her large round eyes, her button nose, her full red lips, and her velvet skin. Carmen giggled all the time and liked to play with other children who treated her like a doll and braided her curly hair into numerous little pigtails.

Donna Esmeralda went to mass every morning. This, and her fame as a foster mother, caused people to consider her as a saint. His wife's saintliness was rather awkward, however, for poor Mylorde. She used to wake him up every morning before going to church, and he had an endless day in front of him with time heavy on his hands. He didn't like to read--not even a newspaper; he had no hobbies which would have been difficult in Donna Esmeralda's spotless home, so he wandered all day long from bar to bar, watching the people and giving his cherished advice.

I have no idea of Mylorde's occupation before he retired, but I assume that he was a kind of broker because he liked business deals. As often as not, his seemingly altruistic counsel involved a substantial kickback for himself. By the way, it was he who told Willy about the bar and extolled its values, and now it was he who introduced prospective buyers to us.

He tried his hand also at matchmaking and had engineered Jussuf's engagement. He knew about the best buys in houses and terrenos and how you could make a fast buck.

Mylorde rarely paid for his drinks, nor did he treat his cronies who ordered drinks for him. When nobody was around to stand him a drink, he ordered a cafezinho. On the other hand, he could consume quantities of hard liquor without showing any sign of intoxication except a darkening of his leathery skin.

When Willy returned from church, Mylorde was balancing his empty cup on his knee. Without a word, Willy took the cup and refilled it with a shot of pinga which Mylorde accepted as his due without a word of thanks.

Willy now stayed in the bar, while Wolfi and I went to church.

Angela grabbed two sweetrolls and a glass of milk while the two boys ran out to loiter in the feira.

When Wolfi and I returned from mass, Sezinho stood already in front of the bar to go shopping with me. He used to carry my shopping bags for a small tip when I bought our family's provisions for the week.

It was around eleven thirty when we came back. Usually I went home afterwards to cook a great dinner, the only meal in the week for which we sat down together, but the bar was so full that Willy asked me to stay and help a little.

The bambino was playing with his friends in the street. His good Sunday suit was already covered with dirt. Angela sold ice cream, Enrico sold candy, and Wolfi dispensed drinks from behind the counter.

"Please mix me a *caipirinha*," I asked him as I began to wash the dishes.

Caipirinha is a popular drink, made of rum, sugar and lime juice. I drank the whole glass in one gulp and soon felt warm and comfortable inside.

After I finished the dishes I left the bar to go home. At the top of the Rua Bonita I paused, as was my custom, to enjoy the great view that gave its name to our suburb. Alta Vista was built on a hill high above the plateau of São Paulo. The river Tietê could be seen as a silvery band where it was not hidden by buildings.

The skyline of the city was forever changing as new highrise buildings popped up like mushrooms, dwarfing the spires of the numerous churches that had formerly dominated it. Behind the city rose the blue mountains that formed the southern border of the plateau. The air was translucent under the soft light of the winter sun. The sky was a cloudless soft blue. I would have liked living here if I had not been a prisoner of the bar.

Just as I intended to resume my way, I heard Willy's sharp voice.

"Annemarie, please come back, we need your help."

They needed help, because a group of about ten people had arrived and wanted something to eat. They had ordered drinks, snacks, and *churasco,* the thin Brazilian steaks fried on the griddle. They had joined the three tables and sat down for a leisurely meal.

While I fried the churasco, our regular patrons arrived and greeted each other in the Brazilian manner by slapping each other's backs while they embraced. If you saw each other every day, you didn't have to go through the whole rigamarole of embracing and back slapping; you simply shook hands. But we had many clients who came only Sundays like Willy's cousin Franz, who was called Chico Almão, and the boyfriend of Sezinho's sister, Senhor Alberto.

Since the chairs were occupied, the men stood all around the counter.

Two groups formed quickly. Senhor Alberto had to pound the backs of the members of both groups, then he joined the group that had formed around Senhor Abraham.

Senhor Abraham was a strange, contradictory man. He was not very tall and had a mighty potbelly, but he gave the impression of a powerful physique because he had broad shoulders which he carried erect, and long muscular arms and hands. He had close cropped black hair, a black mustache, a big nose and twinkling small eyes in a round face. His eyes seemed to imply, "Don't take everything I say at face value."

He was a very rich man. He owned a flourishing shoe shop on our block in the avenida. He was also the landlord of a string of houses in the Rua Bonita that he rented for good money to poor people. His wife, the patient Donna Rachel, took care of the houses. Most of his children were married; only the youngest, Wolfi's friend, Danny, lived at home. Danny worked during the day at the store and went to school at night.

Senhor Abraham was one of the few capitalists in our neighborhood, but he was also a card carrying member of the Communist Party of Brazil.

"As you all know," I heard him say in his booming voice, "there is no unemployment in Russia."

"Vai tomar banyo," take a bath, said Senhor Carlos, the watchmaker. "In Russia you wouldn't have your shoe store, nor your houses and I wouldn't have my shop."

"Patricio," answered Senhor Abraham, "even in Russia people need shoes, and somebody has to fit them; and even in Russia people need watches and watches need repairs."

He paused, took a gulp from his glass. As nobody reacted to his statement, he continued.

"Who says that I would like to live in Russia? All my family left Russia when I was a little boy back in the time of the Tsars. I am a Brasilero, and I love this beautiful country. What I want to bring about is a government of social justice without corruption, in which the people share the natural wealth, and where the masses are not exploited by a few millionaires and foreigners."

"You may be right with your ideals, but I do not want to have a bloody revolution. All I want is a government that isn't corrupt. I think our new mayor, Janio Quadros, is on the right track."

"He will not succeed because he is only a small cog in a system that is rotten to the core."

"I still believe in Janio and his broom with which he wants to sweep São Paulo clean," said Senhor Moses, Senhor Abraham's older brother who owned the furniture store. "My wife told me that the tomatoes are already cheaper since he cleaned up the mess in the Mercado Central."

"That's nothing but eyewash. That's like patching up a deep bullet wound with a bandaid," replied the Communist. "As long as half the population works for the minimum salary that is not enough to buy food for a family, we need radical change."

"Yes," piped in Toninho the greengrocer, "the rich are getting richer, and the poor are getting poorer all the time."

"Senhor Abraham," said the watchmaker, "what do you want? You are one of them who gets richer all the time."

"You yourself will lose everything when the revolution comes that you fight for," said Abraham's brother.

"That's where you are wrong," said Senhor Abraham triumphantly. "*You* will lose everything, when the inevitable revolution comes. But *I* will lose nothing because I am one of them who make the revolution."

While I listened to them the churascos nearly burned. I had to serve my customers who also ordered a new round of drinks. Since I had to prepare the drinks in another part of the bar, I listened now to the conversation of the other group.

The disk jockey, Senhor Nair, was dominating that group. Mylorde had left his throne and stood with the others. Even Jussuf was with them. I was surprised to see Jussuf in the bar instead of taking care of his booth. Maybe the grief over his lost girl drove him to drink. Willy stood with them instead of working, a glass in his hand. Suddenly, Jussuf took something black and shiny out of his hip pocket. They all inspected it closely, as it went from hand to hand. Shortly after it got back to Jussuf, we heard a loud bang. Panthera Negra, who sunned herself on the other side of the Rua Bonita, got startled and ran away.

"You damned idiot," I screamed, "You nearly shot the cat."

Enrico and the bambino howled at the top of their voices while Jussuf put the gun back in his pocket.

"Calma, calma, Annemarie. Don't get excited," said Willy soothingly. "He missed the cat; no harm was done."

"Let's see the gun again," said Senhor Nair.

Jussuf took the pistol again from his pocket, removed the cartridge, and gave it to Enrico.

"Stop crying, here, look what I give you."

The bambino continued to howl. "Sorry," said Jussuf. "I didn't want to kill your cat. I shot above her head. I only wanted to show that it is working."

"I want the gun," said the bambino.

"You can't have it, there are bullets in it," said Jussuf. Then he turned to the men, and asked, "Whose turn is it to pay for the next round?"

"It's your turn," said Mylorde. "But if you don't have money, you can pay with the gun."

"Are you loco?" Jussuf was alarmed. "The gun is worth many

rounds of drinks. I took it from a client who had run up a large debt."

Mylorde eyed the gun with greed. "I know what we will do. We will gamble for it. We all put money in. We will play *fosforos.* The winner will get the gun, but has to pay for the drinks; you, Jussuf, get the money."

"I want to keep the gun," insisted Jussuf.

"What do you need a gun for?" asked the disk jockey. "You don't want to shoot anybody, or do you? Let's all have a chance at it."

This was interesting. I hastened to deliver the drinks to my customers and returned where I could watch the proceedings.

Jussuf was still reluctant, but Mylorde coaxed him. "We will all ante up enough to make it worthwhile for you."

Reluctantly, Jussuf put the gun on top of the counter. After some hassling, everybody put up his stake. Jussuf took the money and put it in his pocket. I gave them a box of matches and each man took two of them. Now the game started. Each man had to take one, two, or no matches in his right fist, and stretch it out. When all the fists were outstretched, each man took his turn to guess the total of the matches in the fists. No number could be used more than once. Then the number of the matches was counted. The one who came nearest to the actual number without going over was declared the winner.

Willy became the proud owner of the gun. He looked at it with disdain. "What can I do with it? I need a gun like a hole in the head."

"You could keep it in the bar to frighten thieves."

"No, I might kill somebody; that's worse than stealing. I don't want to have a gun."

"But you still have to pay for the next round."

"The hell I will," said Willy. "We can play again and your ante will pay for the drinks. You don't have to put in as much as the first time."

I directed my attention again to my customers while Senhor Abraham and his group joined the gamblers.

"You cannot play for nothing," shouted Jussuf. "You have to pay me first."

My customers finally finished their meal, paid and left. I was free to go home. But instead, I sent Angela home with the boys and told her to cook dinner. I filled a waterglass full of pinga for myself and watched the game. I would have liked to gamble with them, but this was a man's game, and it would have been bad manners to join them.

They must have played many rounds, and the gun had changed owners many times, but they enjoyed themselves while Wolfi and I filled their glasses again and again.

I was interrupted by Chico who came in to buy milk, bread and cigarettes. Chico never drank with the other men. He was very shy, nearly a hermit. He lived together with his friend Emilio in the apartment above the bank on the other side of the avenida. We did not know much about the two although Willy rode every day with Emilio to the city. Emilio was a young man like millions of others without any special features that you could remember. You saw him, and two minutes later you forgot his face. You didn't forget Chico, once you had seen him. He was very delicate, with long, blond curls, a red mouth and very small hands and feet. His eyes were blue, with long lashes, and when he dressed up as a girl during the carnival, we all took him for a pretty girl and recognized him only when he started talking.

Chico had no job. He stayed home, kept house for the two and did all the shopping. He was always carefully dressed with razor-sharp creases in his pants and open-necked, freshly laundered white shirts. His hair was well brushed, his face clean shaved and his hands well manicured.

When Chico was ready to leave the bar, he saw the gun and his face lit up. He watched the game for a while. Then he asked timidly, "May I join?"

"Of course," said Willy.

"But you must pay the original ante," insisted Jussuf, and pocketed the money that Chico put on the counter. Jussuf had realized by now that he had a good thing going and did not want to let an opportunity go by.

Chico did not win the first game but ordered his drink like the rest of them. He took a *rabo de gallo,* a rooster's tail, a cocktail made from vermouth and pinga.

"Give me a lot of vermouth with a little pinga," he said to Wolfi.

The game went on and on. Willy forgot his role as the boss of the bar and played with his patrons while Wolfi and I did the work.

It was already half past twelve when the professora sailed in. She was already unsteady on her feet, and her usually olive colored face was flushed to a livid violet. Her heavy body swayed like a ship from side to side, and her long, straight hair fell into her face. She must have been in many bars before she came to us. She ordered a rabo de gallo and sat heavily down.

I filled a glass for myself too and sat down next to the professora to take her weekly order. She was our star customer. Even if she drank day and night, she would not be able to consume all the liquor she ordered. But she had guests, and on many nights we could hear the shouting and chanting from her house.

"Sezinho can carry the things home," she said. "But let him not carry the whole load at one time. It is too much for him to carry. He is not very strong. "

Donna Linda was a very considerate person; even in her drunken stupor, she would not forget the welfare of her friends. Her drunkenness showed in a sentimental benevolence towards the whole world, with kisses and embraces for everyone.

She taught third grade in the elementary school of Alta Vista, and both students and parents loved and respected her for her fairness, her interest in her pupils, and her ability to teach. It was hard to reconcile her basic goodness and intelligence with her uncontrollable alcoholism.

I still sat with the professora when Roberta shuffled in. She was well dressed for a change in a skirt and a clean white blouse. Only her shoes were dirty and down at the heels, and her lipstick was smeared beyond her lips.

Noticing her respectable appearance, I whispered to the professora, "Look how neat she is today. Today is the third Sunday of the month. She always visits her daughter on the third Sunday."

"The dirty whore," murmured the professora under her breath. Then she shouted with the volume of a bullhorn, *"Putah!"*

Putah is the Brazilian word for prostitute, but it is casually used in every fight between women. In Roberta's case, however, it was true.

"Cabeça de vaca," you head of a cow, replied Roberta, which was parried by the professora with *"Cachorra,"* you bitch. Roberta made a comeback with another cussword that was beyond my vocabulary.

Since the Brazilian men are quite polite and would rarely cuss in the presence of a lady, my stock of dirty words was limited mostly to those Wolfi used to show his masculinity. This is the reason why I did not understand half of the ensuing word battle between the two amazons.

The men interrupted their game to listen and to watch the two hyenas. The professora had gotten up, and I tried to steer them towards the rear of the bar. Finally they stood in the narrow passage between the washroom and the store room. Words had given place to actual violence. They scratched each other's face and pulled each other's hair.

At last Roberta left the bar, her head held high with a tuft of long hair in her hand. She had to pass through a throng of bystanders in the street, who, attracted by the shouting, had watched the fight with fascination. Sezinho was among them.

Donna Linda went to the toilet to wash the blood from her face and to arrange her hair. When she returned, she saw the gun on the counter. Her eyes gleamed when she saw it. She asked whether it was for sale. The men explained to her the rules of the game. She paid in, gambled and drank with the others.

I had had enough. I was still nauseated from seeing the blood of the fight. I waited a while until I felt steady enough on my feet because I did not want them to see how drunk I was. I slipped behind the counter to wash the dishes but gave up after I broke two glasses. The men were so drunk that they didn't notice me as I passed by. The gun had disappeared from the counter.

At home, Angela had a good dinner of roast beef, potatoes and salad waiting for us.

"Angela, you're a real angel," I told her. "Thanks a lot. Please keep the food warm until Daddy comes home. I want to wash and rest a little before dinner."

I doubt that Angela noticed how drunk I was; she was a trusting dear thing. I took a shower with lukewarm water which helped me to sober up before dinner.

Willy came half an hour later, and we all sat down to eat. Only Wolfi was not with us because he had to keep the bar open to serve the *merchands* of the feira who took a drink before going home and to sell ice cream and candy to the children who went to the matinee in the movie theater.

"Wolfi said it was alright with him," mentioned Willy. "He wanted to listen to the footbal game of the Corinthians against the team from Minas Gerais on the radio."

It was already two-thirty. "Can we go to the movies this afternoon?" asked Enrico.

"You may, if you can—that is, if there's a film that the censor has given free for the children."

"Oh yes, Mama," volunteered Angela. "The film is not censored. It's the 'Count of Monte Christo.' I want to see it very badly because we have seen the Chateau d'If in Marseille on our way to Brazil."

Angela and Enrico left. I put the bambino to bed for his nap. Then I went to bed too. I would have liked to talk to Willy about the morning in the bar and about my fears concerning Wolfi and Roberta, but he snored already, and I did not have the heart to wake him up.

Enrico's first communion.

Chapter Two

SUNDAY AFTERNOON, JUNE 20

I would have liked to ask Willy whether he knew who got the handgun at the end of the game. But it was not important enough to wake him up. I couldn't sleep because I was worried about our life.

We had come to Brazil with such great hopes of a new and better life. We had left Germany because we were afraid to be trapped between America and Russia in a third World War. Two world wars in one life time were enough for us.

Willy was an unwilling soldier during the war. He returned from the Russian front unhurt except for some frozen toes that had to be amputated, but as a frantic pacifist. Brazil seemed to us distant enough from a possible theater of war. Since Willy had a gift for learning foreign languages easily, we expected that he would find work as translator or interpreter. His work as a cost accountant in Germany seemed to be also a good preparation for our new life. I had studied to be a teacher before our marriage and hoped to continue my education in Brazil.

In order to preserve our limited funds, we bought tickets for the third class in an old and decrepit ship, the *SS Florida,* which sailed from Marseille to South America.

We were not prepared for the stark reality of an emigrant ship. When we saw the immense dormitories in the hold of the ship where sixteen hundred people slept, we had the eerie feeling that such things happen only in books or the movies, not to us. It was the same feeling that we experienced when we came one morning out of the air raid shelter to see our house turned into rubble. But just as we became accustomed to living in one room in Germany, so we got used to sleeping in a dormitory with four hundred people snoring and tossing and suffering from seasickness.

The first weeks in São Paulo were like a beautiful dream. But I had not time for happy reminiscence. I had more important things to do.

I waited until it was time for me to return to the bar. I woke up the bambino and dressed him because he had to stay with me in the bar. I grabbed a couple of toys for him and we left the house. Panthera stood in front of the house, and the bambino took her in his arms.

I walked in front, while the bambino with the cat followed behind. About three steps before we reached the bar, somebody was lying in the street. It was Roberta.

"Come, bambino, Roberta lies in the middle of the street. She must have been completely drunk that she fell down."

I grabbed him and took him in my arms together with the cat and carried them to the bar.

Wolfi had the radio on full force because he was listening to the football game.

He was quite excited. "Mama, imagine, the Corinthians have already shot three goals, and the other team has only one!"

"Great," I said without much enthusiasm, although I had a heavy bet on the Corinthians.

"You know," added Wolfi, "when the Corinthians shot the second goal, somebody shot a fire cracker in the Rua Bonita. It was quite loud and sounded like Jussuf's pistol this morning."

"There are a lot of fireworks in June in this country. You must be used to it by now."

"But Mama, nobody is in the street on a Sunday afternoon. I heard no voices or steps."

"By the way, Wolfi, do you know who had the gun at the end?"

"No idea. Mylorde won the last game. Or rather, when he won, he said, that's the last game. He wanted to take it, but it was no more on the counter."

"And then?"

"Then they looked at each other, and everybody said he didn't have the gun. Then they all left except Jussuf. He sat down, put his head on the table, and fell asleep."

"Where is Jussuf now?"

"He woke up when I turned on the radio. He looked kind of funny, like he didn't know where he was. Then he asked for a strong coffee. He drank it, and remembered that he had left his booth in the feira with a little boy, and that he must go and get his things. Then he left."

"Do you want something to eat?"

"No, I made myself some sandwiches and drank a *guarana.*"

"That's fine, but we left you some of the Sunday dinner."

"Fernando and Danny want me to go with them to the dance at the Horto Florestal, and I didn't want to lose time. I am already late."

"If you leave right away you may be able to catch up with them."

"Mama, I am broke; could you give me some money?"

"Of course, you have earned it. But I don't understand how you can be broke, now that you are a wage earner."

"I don't get paid till next Friday." I gave him the money.

"Thanks, I will go home to wash and change. Then I will be on my way."

"Don't get excited when you go home. Roberta is lying in the middle of the street. I don't understand why she could not go home to sleep it off."

"Roberta left long before the others, right after her fight with Donna Linda. You were still here."

"Did you not see her afterwards?"

"No, I closed the door to the Rua Bonita because it was so windy. I couldn't have seen her there."

Wolfi had washed all the dishes, and I had nothing to do in the bar. So I sat down with the Bambino to play with him.

Suddenly we heard a scream in the street and Wolfi ran in, quite shook up.

"Mama, somebody has shot Roberta!"

"Don't joke, such things happen only in books."

"Mama, she is dead. I touched her to wake her up. She is ice cold."

"No, Wolfi, that's impossible. I don't believe it."

"Go look for yourself."

"Take care of the bambino."

"I want to see the dead Roberta. You didn't let me see her when we came up," screamed the bambino.

"That's not a sight for a little boy like you."

I went out while Wolfi held the little boy who was wriggling in his arms.

Wolfi was right. Roberta was dead in the middle of the street, in full daylight, while all the inhabitants of Vila Alta Vista were in bed or in the movie theater or God knows where.

It was obvious that Roberta had been home after her bout with the professora. She still wore the same skirt but had changed her blouse and washed her face. Her light blue blouse was bloodstained and under her body, the gray dust of the unpaved street was dyed an ugly brown.

She was lying on her left side with her right arm in front of her face as if she wanted to shield herself, but her wide open eyes seemed to stare at me accusingly. Her purse must have fallen from her hand. It was open and its contents were scattered in the street.

I cautiously touched her hand. It was cold and stiff. Then I closed the accusing eyes. I felt nauseated as always when I saw blood. Suddenly, a wave of pity flowed over me for her short futile life. I had tears in my eyes when I stood up again.

"I'll have to tell the police that I touched the corpse. Wolfi must also. Otherwise we'll have troubles," I told myself.

I looked at the mess in the street in order to form a clear mental picture of everything I saw so that I would be able to testify about it later.

The objects near her body included her open purse, her workbook—used as an identification in Brazil, a dirty handkerchief very much in contrast to her clean blouse, a lipstick, a vial with perfume, a large box of candy, a box with color crayons, and a little box of condoms.

I did not touch anything but left it where I had found it and returned to the bar.

"Wolfi," I said, "you will have to go to the police station and tell them that we have a corpse in our street. I think it is best that you take the Bambino with you because I do not want to have him here. I am sorry that your afternoon is spoiled."

"Don't be so unconcerned. What does it matter if my afternoon is spoiled when the poor girl is dead. I don't understand you, Mama. I could cry when I think that she was still so much alive this morning."

"I want to see Roberta," cried the Bambino, but Wolfi swept him into his arms and ran away.

I sat down and wrote a list of the articles that I had seen in the street. I went out again to make sure that I had not forgotten anything and found her wallet, half hidden by the purse. I looked into the purse. It was empty.

When I got back into the bar, I poured myself a stiff dose of pinga. I was altogether alone. Nobody was in the ghostly street, only an occasional car or bus passed in the avenida. Outside lay the girl that I had hated while she was alive and for whom I was sorry now that she was dead.

As a matter of fact, I knew her quite well, and I knew that she was not as bad as the people believed. In order to judge her, it was necessary to know her life story and how she became a prostitute. This is her story as I reconstructed it from bits and pieces that she told me while visiting with me in the bar, when neither of us had any customers.

Roberta called herself proudly "a *Portuguesa,*" although she had dark skin and kinky hair because her father was a Portuguese. She must have been a pretty girl because she had regular features, a finely chiseled face with large eyes, a small nose, a well-formed mouth, and a round chin.

When she laughed, she showed shining white teeth. But nowadays her face was swollen and sallow and her large eyes were bloodshot.

Basically, she had a nice figure, but it was usually hidden under her torn and shapeless sweater. Her shoes, even today in her Sunday finery, were down at the heel, and her stockings were sagging. She never wore a girdle or a bra.

Roberta did not know much about her white father, the boyfriend of her negro mother, not even his name. He was a wealthy merchant whose wife was barren. He told Roberta that she was his one and only daughter.

Roberta thought that her father might have married her mother if he had been able to because he was good to her, and they seemed to love each other. But there is no divorce in Brazil because the all-powerful Catholic Church prevented a law permitting divorce from being passed.

Like so many Brazilians, Roberta's father led a double life. He spent the week with his espoused wife as a respected business man, and during the weekend, he visited the woman he loved for a few precious moments of fulfillment. It was an arrangement like the one between Senhor Alberto and Sezinho's sister.

Roberta had only good recollections about her father, who treated her and her mother with love and respect. He paid for a nice house with decent furniture for them. Roberta went to school until fourth grade and knew how to read and write. But, unfortunately, her mother was a warmblooded creature, and a man in bed only once a week was not enough for her.

One day she ran away with a strapping young man, and Roberta never heard from her again. When her father arrived the next weekend, he found a sad girl on the doorstep and an empty bed. He was very disappointed, but he paid for one week the rent of the house and left money with Roberta to buy her food.

He told Roberta that she could not live by herself. He would come back next week and arrange for her to go to a boarding school. Boarding school, for Roberta, meant orphanage. She had heard enough horror stories about beatings and starvation in orphanages to become terrified.

She did not wait for her father's return, nor did she ever get in touch with him. In her mind, he had rejected her, the same as her mother had. She did not remember his name or address, not even what he did for a living. A golden little cross that he once gave her was her only link with the past.

Compulsory education in Brazil ends with fourth grade. Roberta was already twelve years old and had finished elementary school. She easily obtained a *carteiro de trabalho*, a workbook and found work as an unskilled laborer in a shoe factory. She earned the *salario minimo por menores*, the minimum salary for minors which was not enough for one person's modest living expenses. She rented a bed in a dormitory in a rooming house and was often hungry.

After a year or so she found a friend who rented a room for her when he visited her on weekends, like her father had visited her mother. He also bought her pretty dresses. When she got pregnant at the age of fifteen, he even arranged for an abortion by an abortionist with a good reputation for cleanliness. Abortion, though illegal, is, of course, widespread in Brazil, but infections after abortions are also widespread and good abortionists are expensive.

Roberta realized that it was very generous of her friend to pay for such an elaborate abortion. She was even allowed to stay at the doctor's house for a few hours rest before she had to go home. But even as a fifteen year old girl, she felt sorry for the life she had destroyed.

A few years passed in relative quiet and comfort. Then she became pregnant again. When she told her boyfriend about it, she told him also that she wanted to give birth to the child instead of having another abortion. The young man got very angry and beat her cruelly and told her that he was sick and tired of her anyway and that she should find herself another sucker.

Roberta told me that she was kind of relieved when he left her because she wanted the baby all to herself. It was shortly before her eighteenth birthday when she would earn the minimum salary for adults, and she thought this might be enough for her and her baby to live on.

I think that the loss of her job on her eighteenth birthday was worse in her eyes than the loss of her parents. It was a very common story actually. Many factories take advantage of the ridiculously low minimum salary for minors and then let the young workers go when they were eighteen years old. Those youngsters usually have no saleable skill, and I heard many stories similar to Roberta's story while we were in Brazil.

So, Roberta was eighteen years old, unemployed, and five months pregnant. She had nobody to ask for advice except the girls at work. They told her to go to the Rua Cantareira where the prostitutes lived.

When she walked there, a pimp stopped her and asked her what she was doing in his territory. He was not unfriendly, and she told him her story. She also told him that she did not want to abort her baby.

The young man, whom she knew under the name of Toninho, suggested that she could work as a maid in his "rooming house," where her daughter Innocencia was born in due time.

While she was pregnant, Roberta went to church. It seems that she even went to confession because she told me that the priest lauded her for not aborting her baby. Other than this one remark, Roberta never touched the topic of religion. She wore the cross that was given to her by her father, but I did not know whether this was a gesture of family sentimentality or a gesture of religion.

I asked her why she had called her daughter Innocencia. "I felt that my life was so dirty, and I wanted her to lead an innocent life."

This showed me that she might have had misgivings about her style of life. But when Toninho offered to let her become a full-fledged whore, she accepted.

Toninho arranged the deal with the foster parents for Innocencia and the monthly visits by her mother. Innocencia was still with the same foster parents when I knew Roberta. Roberta paid for her expenses during her visit to the child every third Sunday of the month.

I knew about Roberta only through her own words and only what she wanted me to know. She never spoke about the years in the bordello during which the eager, pretty, young girl changed into a prematurely aged, alcoholic slattern.

Roberta did not leave the whore house voluntarily. Janio Quadros, the young and energetic new mayor of São Paulo, fulfilled his pledge to clean up the city with his broom by pouncing down on the Rua Cantareira.

His anti-vice squads arrested pimps and prostitutes and closed their establishments. Roberta was with her daughter the day they raided her place. When she returned, the house was boarded up, and neighbors told her that Toni and the ladies were in prison. She could not even take her belongings out of the house.

She finally came to Vila Alta Vista and rented the little room with the private entrance in Senhor Carlos' back yard where she now lived, cooked, drank, and plied her trade.

It seemed that her business was good because I saw many men enter the courtyard of her room.

Whenever I watched the entrance to Roberta's den of vice, I could not help imagining Wolfi on his way to Roberta's inferno.

This danger was over now. Roberta was dead. I was pouring myself another pinga to toast the passing of this danger when I saw our friend Kurt getting out of the bus. Kurt was the companion of our Sunday excursions before we were shackled to the bar, and still liked to visit us on Sunday afternoons.

Today, as was his custom, Kurt had his camera with him. He had brought also the pictures of Enrico's First Communion which he wanted to show me. He was quite disappointed that I did not show any interest in looking at the pictures; instead, I interrupted him.

"Kurt, imagine, Roberta has been shot."

Kurt looked at me uncomprehendingly because he did not know how to react.

"Which Roberta?"

"Roberta was the whore of Alta Vista. Somebody shot her this afternoon. She lies right outside the bar. Wolfi went to get the police. Go, and have a look, but do not touch anything."

Kurt went out, but he returned right away to get his camera to make a series of pictures of the scene of the crime and the corpse. It was nearly four-thirty and dusk was settling, but Kurt thought he had enough light to take pictures with his sensitive camera.

When he had finished I told him, "Kurt, it is getting quite chilly. Please stay in the bar while I go home and get something warm for me and the kids. I'll be back soon."

"Sure thing," said Kurt. "Do you think I can sell the pictures?"

"Try the *Folhas.*"

The *Folhas,* the "Leaves" of São Paulo had a large circulation. It was the only afternoon paper and was famous for its immense want-ads section, its sensational stories, and its editorials against the shortcomings of the establishment. The paper was bought by practically everybody who knew how to read.

While I was going down the Rua Bonita, Sezinho was on his way up.

"Nossa Senhora Apparecida," he screamed when he saw the corpse."I must go and tell the professora."

But he remained in front of the dead girl as if he was paralyzed. I looked back while rounding the corner and saw him bending down towards the corpse.

"I hope he doesn't touch anything, I thought. But anyway, it's none of my business."

Willy was in the bathroom when I got home, getting ready to return to the bar.

"Roberta was shot; she lies in the middle of the street in front of the bar," I blurted out without any preamble.

"Don't get always so excited," said Willy, very unfriendly. "Calm down, and tell me what has happened."

His constant advice to calm down was like a red cape for me.

"Heck, you would also get excited if you had seen a corpse in the street."

I went to gather the sweater and was ready to leave when he came after me.

"Let's sit down. Then you can tell me all about it."

We sat down at the kitchen table with a glass of pinga each while I told him how I saw her first and thought she was sleeping, and how Wolfi saw that she was dead and that I had sent Wolfi to the police station with the Bambino; that as far as I knew only Kurt and Sezinho had seen the corpse and that Kurt was in the bar.

"Do you remember who had the gun at the end?"

Willy tried to remember. "No, I haven't the slightest idea. But how do you know that she has been shot with Jussuf's gun?"

"She could have been shot with any gun. But it is a coincidence that we had a gun in the bar. The police will want to know about it. Actually, I do not remember having seen a gun near her. Please come with me to the bar before the police arrive."

"I'll be ready in five minutes. Can you wait so long?"

I was too impatient to wait. I grabbed the sweaters and ran back to the bar without looking at the scene of the crime.

Several people stood around the dead girl, and the professora puffed behind me as she went uphill. When I was about to enter the bar, I turned and shouted.

"You people, you better leave this place before the police come."

They followed me into the bar, and I sold them pinga and cafezinhos.

At last the squad car arrived with the sirens going full blast. There were four officers in uniform as well as Wolfi and the Bambino. The latter was quite excited about his ride and imitated the sirens for quite a while.

The four policemen looked at the corpse and dispersed the people that had collected again.

"Nobody should touch anything before the homicide people arrive from headquarters," shouted the commanding officer.

He dispatched the squad car with one man to call homicide, while he and the other two men entered the bar.

I asked Wolfi why it had taken them so long to come. He said that only one officer was in the police station; all the others had gone to investigate a car pile-up near the Horto Florestal . . . as soon as they returned, they took off with the children.

I had my hands full because all the bystanders were now in the bar. The officer in charge told them that they could not leave but had to wait until the homicide squad arrived from the city.

The professora had an argument with him. "You must remove the corpse right away because the children will come back from the movies any minute now."

"I cannot do this; the corpse has to stay where it is until the scene of the crime has been investigated."

"But you can't let the children see this mess."

"I'll send one of my men to divert the children, and the other can close the other end of the Rua Bonita."

It was now dark outside. The two policemen were out in the street, and the officer in charge stood in the bar. None of them was near the body of the girl when Willy was on his way to the bar.

He saw an unknown man standing near the corpse. He addressed Willy.

"Now, look at this. There is a corpse lying in the street. She seems to have been dead for quite a while, quite cold and stiff, and

nobody is around. I saw a policeman up in that bar in the avenida, so
they must be aware of the murder. I will teach them a lesson. You
know, I am a reporter for the *Folhas*. I am going to make a big stink
about this. Look what I am going to do so you can testify about it
later." He took the purse while he wrapped a handkerchief around
his hand, took the wallet that lay underneath it, replaced the purse,
and put the wallet in his pocket.

"See how easy it is to rob a corpse in São Paulo. But don't tell
anybody about me until I get my story in the paper."

Willy found this very funny and relished the idea that a trick was
being played on the police. Later, at night, after I had told him that
Roberta used to carry all her money in that wallet, he did not find it
so funny any more. I was sure that she had her money in the wallet
because she would have to pay the fosterparents of her daughter.

Five of our regulars, who had been in the bar during the game
this morning, were now in the bar: Senhor Carlos, Mylorde, Senhor
Alberto, Senhor Nair, and the professora. Emilio, Chico's partner,
Wolfi, Sezinho, and the Bambino were also there and a few people
whom we did not know.

Sezinho played with the Bambino on one of the tables, and I
noticed that his hands trembled as he tried to make a tower with
the Bambino's building blocks.

There was now noise and commotion in the avenida. The crowd
from the movie theater trouped through. Normally, some of them
would have stopped at the bar to buy ice cream, but the cops did not
let them enter.

"Mama, the cops wouldn't let us go home," cried Enrico as he
stormed into the bar.

"I know," I said as calmly as I could. "Roberta had an accident
in the Avenida."

"Roberta is dead, quite dead," shouted Angela at the top of her
voice.

"How do you know?"

"I slipped past the cops. I saw her. She has a hole in her blouse
and was bloody all over. Enrico saw her too."

I didn't know what to say. I had them put on their sweaters and
prepared sandwiches for them. They were both quite excited and
prattled continuously until Wolfi stopped them.

"Shut up, for Christ's sake. There are other people in the bar."

We all milled around in the bar without saying anything new or
interesting when the sirens screeched. Homicide had arrived at last
from the city. It was now six, a full three hours since the Corinthians
shot their second goal.

Two policemen in uniform and two in mufti entered the bar.
Even before they looked at the scene of the murder, they declared,
"Nobody is allowed to leave this place before we have interviewed

him."

Then, they went out to take pictures and fingerprints. The avenida was now full with people, but nobody was permitted to go near the scene of the crime or to enter the bar. It seemed to be an eternity until the ambulance arrived. They put the body in, and the two uniformed men left with the ambulance.

"I am Captain Alfredo from police headquarters and my colleague is a fingerprint expert and investigator," one of the two introduced himself. He wore an elegant sports coat, a striped shirt and a wild, multicolored tie. He was tall and held himself erect. His shoulders were broad, or at least heavily padded; he had slick, shining black hair, a small mustache, large liquid eyes and regular features. He looked like a white-skinned man with a healthy tan—in short, he was dashingly handsome and very aware of his sex appeal. I must admit that I was impressed by his appearance.

He asked who the owner of the establishment was and then addressed Willy.

"Would you be so kind as to let us interview these people in your place? Otherwise I would have to take them all to headquarters."

"We have a store room at the rear of the bar. You could put a table and chairs in it, and use it. Nobody will disturb you there."

Captain Alfredo went to the store room with all its cases of full and empty bottles and said that it would suit him fine.

The three policemen from Alta Vista were all in the bar by now. Captain Alfredo sent his colleague with one of them back to the Alta Vista police station and kept two of them in the bar. They put a table and two chairs in the storeroom. Then one of them stayed in the doorway to the avenida, the other next to the door to the storeroom. The door to the Rua Bonita had been closed since noon.

Captain Alfredo sat down in the storeroom and called the people in, one by one. After the interview, each of them had to leave the bar without talking with anybody who was in the bar.

I forgot to say that Kurt had left as soon as I came back to the bar with the sweaters because he wanted to develop his pictures right away. Nobody mentioned Kurt, or his pictures.

Captain Alfredo called first the people who said they didn't know Roberta. Only one of the people I didn't know admitted that he knew her. Except for him, the others left after a very short interview. He probably took only their names and addresses. The one who knew Roberta stayed for about ten minutes with the captain. Then it was Emilio's turn. Emilio didn't stay very long. He wasn't in the bar during the morning and had come to the bar only a few minutes before the police arrived.

I was surprised that he admitted that he knew the prostitute because I was under the impression that he was not interested in the female sex.

The other people stayed each about twenty minutes in the store-room with the captain. The longest interview was the one with Wolfi. It was he who had found the corpse, who knew the time of the crime, who had called the police, and he was also all morning long in the bar and probably described the gambling for the gun. God knows what he told the captain. He liked to embellish stories, and to aggrandize himself. His face was red when he emerged at last.

Since I was not allowed to talk with him, I asked the policeman whether the children could go home with him. He conferred with Captain Alfredo and let them go.

Finally only Willy and I were left. I asked Willy again whether he remembered who had the weapon at the end of the morning session, but he did not know.

Then he was called in and I stayed alone with the two cops. It was cold and clammy in the bar. I offered them a pinga, and they accepted gratefully. I sat down with them and had a pinga myself. They were impatient because it was long past their shift, and they were tired and wanted to go home. Their shift was from twelve to eight, and it was already past ten o'clock.

As Willy told me later, he had to go again over every incident that had happened during the morning. He thought that Captain Alfredo was convinced that the murder had been committed with Jussuf's gun and wanted to know the names of all the people who had participated in the game.

Willy waited for me to finish my interview and continued to treat the cops.

Before I even sat down on the chair facing the captain across the table, I gave him a cartridge. It was the one that Jussuf had given Enrico after he had fired on the cat. The captain was grateful for my cooperation and henceforth considered me a friend and helper.

He showed me a list of the people that Willy had mentioned and I added Sezinho's name to it. I also gave him the list of the articles that I had seen scattered around the body in the street. He read it carefully and mentioned that his people had seen neither the wallet, nor the candy, nor the color crayons. At that time I did not yet know about the reporter of the *Folhas,* and I volunteered the information that Roberta must have had a fairly large amount of money in her wallet.

I also told him that Sezinho stayed for a while near the body of the girl, and that I had seen that he stooped down to it.

I really didn't want to throw any suspicion on the little boy, but I felt it was important that the captain knew about it. However, he didn't seem to give it much weight at the time.

He asked me to tell him all that I knew about Roberta. I told him most of what I knew, leaving out my fears about Wolfi. I tried my best to paint her in a favorable light.

I talked about her devotion to her little girl. She always carried a picture of her pretty daughter in her wallet which she showed off with much pride. Whenever she visited little Innocencia, she brought presents to her. I often watched her in the feira when she bought a doll or a pretty dress.

I also told him how helpful Roberta tried to be. Several times she slipped behind the counter to help me to wash the dirty dishes. I did not tell him about the aversion I felt whenever our bodies touched each other.

Then I recalled an incident that happened not so long ago. It was around two in the afternoon; Wolfi was still in school, and Angela was on a school picnic because it was the last day before vacation. I was alone with the two boys in the bar. They were both quite unruly because they were hungry, and I had no time to fix them anything because I had just received a large shipment of bottled drinks that stood on the floor and had to be carried to the storeroom.

Just then Roberta shuffled in to get her early morning drink. She was dressed in dirty rags with sagging stockings and her old slippers. She had lipstick smeared all over her face, her hair was uncombed and she smelled unwashed. She was friendly as always and asked me what was wrong with the children. I told her that they were hungry because I had no time to fix their lunch. Roberta left the bar without a word and without drinking the pinga that I had poured for her. I shrugged my shoulders and poured the pinga down the drain because I didn't want to drink from her glass.

Finally I finished my work and made sandwiches for the boys. When we sat down at last to eat, Roberta came in again, carrying a dish with warmed up rice and beans.

"Somebody who is so considerate cannot be altogether evil," I finished my story.

Captain Alfredo asked more questions about our patrons, and he also asked me whether I knew who were Roberta's customers. I replied that I did not know and couldn't care less. I was so tired that it must have shown in my face.

"That's all for tonight," he said finally. "You look tired and can tell me the rest tomorrow. It seems that you had a long day."

"Yes, it was quite a day, and I am very tired."

"I want to thank you," he said finally, and shook my hand. "You were extremely helpful."

After the captain had left with the two cops, Willy and I pulled down the shutters and went home. We saw that the squad car had come back to pick up the captain and his cops.

On the way back home, Willy told me about the reporter and what a good story it would be.

"Maybe it wasn't a reporter at all, but the murderer who had returned for the money," I mused.

"Quite possible," agreed Willy.

The children were fast asleep when we came home, and we went to bed, too, and fell asleep right away.

The ice cream machine with Annemarie, the Bambino and a customer.

Chapter Three

MONDAY, JUNE 21

The alarm clock rang at six thirty. I didn't have to wake the children because they had their winter vacation and could sleep as long as they wanted. I had to be in the bar before seven although the first customers did not come before eight.

I needed one hour to clean the bar, to take care of the empty bottles, to make coffee and to talk with Panthera about yesterday's events. I did not open the shutter to the Rua Bonita because I didn't want to see the ugly brown stain, and because it was too chilly.

Willy came earlier than usual for his breakfast because he felt the need for a chat with me.

"Do you have any theory about the murder?" he asked me while munching his sandwich.

"I don't know what to say. Any of our friends might have done it. Sezinho is fully convinced that it was the professora."

"Because of their fight?"

"Not only that. He knows that yesterday was not their first fight. Of course, the other times they just shouted at each other, but he knew that the professora hated Roberta's guts. The professora tells everybody who is willing to listen that it is a shame to have a whore living next door, and that we should unite to drive her out."

"Are you a willing disciple of hers?"

"Kind of; I certainly didn't cherish her company."

"Let the one who is without blame throw the first stone. I don't mean you, but the professora is not an innocent angel herself."

"Do you think the professora was afraid of competition?" I asked surprised. I never connected the professora with sexual irregularities.

"Don't be so naive. The professora is not a prostitute. She has a different racket. The noise from her house comes from their *macumba* sessions."

Macumba is the Brazilian version of voodoo, a strange mixture of African, Indian, and Christian rituals and ceremonies that are usually combined with lavish consumption of alcohol. They practised spiritualism and necromancy.

"You're right, of course, but she got always very emotional when she talked about Roberta. Sezinho knows also that she gambled for the gun. I guess he has seen the gun in her hand."

"Do you yourself think that it was the professora? There were other people who hated the girl."

"I suspect nobody, but tell me who is your first choice as suspect?"

"It is just a wild guess, and I am probably wrong. But Senhor Abraham was upset about Roberta. Because he thought that Danny had something to do with her. Then there is Donna Irma who is jealous because she knows that Nair went to her."

"How would you know about Donna Irma. You never talk to her?"

"Senhor Nair told me that she gives him hell since she knows about his escapade."

"Do you have any other clues?"

"Not about Nair. But did you notice Chico? It was so untypical for him to join us when we gambled. Chico is afraid that Emilio is attracted by her. And what do you think about Jussuf who broke up with his fiancee?"

"I guess everybody is a suspect, except Wolfi, Chico Almao, and you."

"And you, of course," said Willy smiling, and gave me a rare hug.

I would have welcomed another hug, but Emilio called from across the street that a taxi was in sight. Busses did not stop in the avenida during rush hours because they were filled up at the terminal. Willy had to share a service taxi with others to go to work in the mornings. It was quite expensive, but there was no other way.

After Willy was gone, I turned the radio on. It was, of course, Radio Bandeirantes where our friend Nair was the disk jockey during the morning hours. He worked from five till nine on the air, reported the news, spoke the commercials, and played the records. He had a dark, manly voice, a little bit rough from all the alcohol he consumed. He put a personal note into his work and interspersed his talk with personal messages to his friends and fans.

We also told him which records to play. He was in the middle of a commercial for reducing tablets.

"Men hate fat women," he said, and it always hit me at my sore spot when he read this commercial with such deep conviction because

I, myself, was fairly overweight.

After the commercial he continued, "Now I am going to play the record of the *Parachutistas* for my dear friend Sezinho who will be nine years old today."

I made a mental note to wish Sezinho a happy birthday and to give him a present. "He will be here any moment now," I thought.

Many neighborhood children came now to buy their milk, butter and rolls, but Sezinho was none of them. He passed by and made his purchase in the other bar. He had never done this before.

None of our patrons showed up for morning cafezinho. My bar was empty. I stole out to have a look at the other bar. True enough, they were all standing there around the counter, the merchands of the avenida, the bank tellers and the dentists.

Nobody saw me peeking in because they were so absorbed in their conversation.

"The hell with that damned murder," I murmured to myself. "It has ruined all my business."

When I returned to my bar, the radio was still on. Senhor Nair's voice said, "And now I want to play a German record for the poor Donna Anna Maria who had such a bad day yesterday."

This, of course, made me feel better. I liked him again. Senhor Nair da Silva Oliveiro was handsome in a rugged way. He had well-greased, wavy chestnut brown hair and brown, bloodshot eyes under bushy brows. He had a Hitler type mustache, regular features, and a sallow, unhealthy complexion. He was probably of Portuguese descent with other races thrown in, while his wife, Donna Irma, was pure Italian.

Donna Irma had a delicate pale skin and auburn, long hair, a large sensuous mouth, like Sophia Loren, a large nose and large protruding eyes. She was of medium height and had a perfect figure. She wore very decent make-up and was always elegantly, but not extravagantly, dressed. She did not flout her femininity and did not seem interested in attracting other men.

It could have been an ideal marriage. Both of them were attractive people. But they were unhappy. Both of them wanted children, but, as hard as they tried, they could not succeed.

Donna Irma went from one doctor to the other. Every one of them said the same thing—that she was perfectly healthy and they could find no reason why she could not bear children.

Nair, as Donna Irma confided sadly, refused steadfastly to see a doctor in this matter. She did not know why he was so insistent in his refusal. Even when he was sick, he did not let her call a doctor. "They are all phonies," he said. The more Donna Irma urged him to see a doctor, the more obstinate he became.

After her failure with doctors, Donna Irma tried her luck with religion. She spent a lot of money for masses and special prayers and finally made a pilgrimage to the most famous shrine in Brazil, the shrine of Nossa Senhora Apparecida, the Patron Saint of Brazil.

Donna Irma's pilgrimage gave her some emotional relief, but she still did not become pregnant. After Nossa Senhora Apparecida, she consulted a faith healer, but also without results. Finally she gave up hope of having a baby and bought herself a parrot instead whom she taught a few words.

All her latent energy found an outlet in her home which she scrubbed and cleaned from morning to night. Every article in her house—and she collected knick-knacks by the hundreds—was washed, polished and dusted every day. Her floors were slick like skating rinks, and every pillow on the armchairs and the sofa was fluffed to the right appearance, so that it was impossible to sit on them.

Senhor Nair was only allowed to sit in a straight backed chair; he was not allowed to put his feet up, nor to smoke. Only in the kitchen could he eat, drink, or smoke.

Home was like a prison to him. Even Donna Irma's kitchen was unpleasant to him because he did not like Donna Irma's Italian family which crowded the kitchen all day long to taste Donna Irma's sumptuous concoctions. He knew that they didn't like him either, and that they tried to influence Donna Irma against him.

Only once did Senhor Nair unburden his heart to me and complain about Donna Irma and her family. He tried to explain to me that this was the reason for his alcoholism, and for the fact that he spent most of his days wandering from bar to bar.

He returned every morning at ten thirty from the city after he had finished his work, preparing the records for the next day. He never went straight home but made the rounds of several bars until it was time for lunch and his siesta. In the afternoon, he emerged again and continued to wander from bar to bar until it was time for dinner. Even after dinner he used to stand around in our bar and keep Willy company until closing time.

I saw him once in Roberta's doorway. In the bar he would not greet her nor show that he knew her. Donna Irma, however, probably suspected hanky-panky.

I visited Donna Irma's mausoleum from time to time. Donna Irma loved children, and our bambino was one of her pets. The bambino loved her cooking, and he liked to talk to her parrot. When he was with me in the bar, he often ran out to go to Donna Irma's house.

The little boy knew quite well that he was not supposed to cross the avenida, and he never did, but on our side he knew everybody, and everybody knew him. He visited the neighbors and their shops or he played with the little boys of Toninho, the greengrocer.

When I came to Donna Irma in my search for the bambino she usually invited me for a cup of coffee and cake and a shot of liquor.

It was very rare that I was her only visitor, but when she was alone, she unburdened her heart about the great tragedy of her marriage.

Last week she came up with a new plan. She had read in one of her magazines that a man had a better chance to fertilize an egg after a long period of continence. Therefore, she had rationed their sex life to once a week.

I don't like to meddle with other people's lives, but in this instance, I had to give her a piece of my mind.

"Donna Irma, don't play with fire. A man will not stand for this kind of treatment. This will take a bad end."

Donna Irma was alarmed about my words and blurted out, "If Nair was unfaithful to me, I would shoot both him and the woman."

This was before I saw Nair in Roberta's entrance way the other day. If she had followed my advice, the poor man might not have found solace in Roberta's dirty arms. It would serve Donna Irma right, the silly goose.

The bar was still empty when Wolfi showed up for breakfast. He had a part-time job during the vacation in the photo lab of Kurt's friends. He did not earn much—less than the salario minimum for *menores,* but for him it was an escape from the bar, and it was nice to have money in the pocket to invite a girl to the movies or buy himself a shirt of his own choice. He also saved money for the entrance fee to a sports club.

I missed Wolfi in the bar. During the semester he went to school only in the mornings and worked in the bar during my lunch hour and for two afternoons during the week when I went shopping, visited friends or took the two little boys on excursions.

"Wolfi," I asked him hesitantly, "could you please take an afternoon off this week? I have a toothache and have to see the dentist."

His face fell. I knew that he hated to miss a day of work, but he said, "Tomorrow is impossible, but I will try to get off on Wednesday."

I fried two eggs for him and gave him bread, cheese and butter. His mind was busy with yesterday's murder.

"Mama, Senhor Abraham said that they didn't have prostitution in Soviet Russia. When a girl sleeps with a man for money, they shoot her, or send her to Siberia. Could it be he who shot Roberta?"

"No, Wolfi," I said with conviction, "Senhor Abraham meant that the government should prohibit prostitution and take strong measures that the law is enforced, but he would never take the law into his own hands."

But when I thought of my feelings as a mother when I saw Roberta on Wolfi's lap, and the fact that Roberta had received Danny in her room, I realized that Senhor Abraham was one of the people on the suspects list.

"I think that Senhor Abraham is too level-headed to do such a thing."

"But Mama, Senhor Abraham is not so levelheaded as you think. On one hand he is a member of the Communist party and boasts to all of us about it, and on the other hand, he is the worst capitalist and slumlord of Alta Vista."

"Mm," I agreed.

"Donna Aurora, who lives in one of his houses, told us this morning that her roof leaks and that he does nothing to repair it. "Your husband can fix it," he said to her.

"Senhor Abraham does always what he thinks is best for himself and his money. He is convinced that we are going to have a revolution, and he wants to be sure to come out on top of it. But I really don't believe that he would shoot somebody."

Wolfi had to leave suddenly because his bus came in sight. After he left, clients came to the bar, and I had to serve them. But they were not our regular patrons and I didn't talk with them.

Instead I looked after Wolfi as he crossed the avenida. He was so grown up for his fourteen years, and I talked with him about everything under the sun. This was beautiful, yet I would have preferred if he had been more childish and innocent. The life in the bar made him too worldwise. I didn't consider that his friends would have enlightened him anyway.

Mylorde entered the bar shortly afterwards. He didn't order anything, only said "Good morning" and took a chair to sit down outside the bar in the street. He talked to the passers-by, but none of them came in to order drinks.

The fat João, the son of Senhor Ernesto, our landlord, chatted with him for quite a while, but he, too, did not order anything. He was as miserly as his father and always waited for a friend to stand him a drink, the same as Mylorde.

I regarded the young man with mixed feelings. He had a bloated, round face, and thin, dishwater blond hair. He had a receding hairline and would soon be bald. He must have been around thirty years old, but he showed no interest whatsoever in girls, nor, like Chico, in boys. His only interests seemed to be food and football. Even now, he talked with Mylorde about yesterday's football game instead of about the murder. Senhor Ernesto and Donna Anna were very unhappy about João's indifference because they dearly wanted grandchildren.

João would inherit quite a fortune. His father owned not only all the buildings in our block in the avenida with all its shops and apartments, but also a number of one-family houses in the Rua Promirim, where we lived, which was parallel to the avenida and just one block below it.

João was not exactly a bright man, but we all liked him because he was very friendly and had a sweet smile. With his money and his smile, he could have easily found a nice girlfriend.

My thoughts turned to Roberta. Her dream had been a conventional marriage to any man who could offer her a home. She tried her luck with every eligible bachelor. João always blushed when she tried to talk with him, but he was too shy to reply; he just smiled, as friendly as he smiled to everybody.

I remembered that he was also one of the gamblers yesterday. It was out of character for him, but he had put up money for the ante. I saw him in possession of the gun once, but afterwards he lost it again.

Today, he gave me his friendly grin and walked away after his chat with Mylorde who had other company in the meantime. Toninho, the greengrocer ordered pinga for all of them. They all waited for Senhor Nair.

It was half past ten, and I wondered why Angela had not yet come with the boys. But then I remembered that Wolfi had mentioned Aurora. Of course, Monday was the day that Donna Aurora came to wash, iron and to clean the house. The children loved Donna Aurora and Terezinha, her little daughter, whom she always took along. When Donna Aurora came to the house, Angela prepared breakfast for all of them, and they played with Terezinha at home.

Toninho returned the empty glasses and asked me where the children were.

"They play usually at home during vacation," I said.

"Oh yes, I remember," replied Toninho. "My boys also played in your house last week."

Toninho, the Japanese, lived with his diminutive wife, Donna Rita, in an apartment behind the green grocery. They had a great number of tiny boys. Their great wish was to have a little girl, and they worked on it year in, year out, but each of their efforts was crowned with the birth of a little boy.

I wasn't worried about the children—they played in a place under our house which was built on a hill. The front part was on stilts, and the back of the house was on ground level. Under the stilts was an open place. The entrance was high enough for the children to sit, but towards the end it got lower and lower. The floor was covered with old blankets, and they had decorated the place with empty crates. Angela and her friends played with dolls, the boys made models. and now in June, balloons for the feast of St. John. I noticed that more and more of the neighbor children came to play under our house, which made me glad, because Enrico used to complain that he didn't have any friends.

Right now I was fully occupied in the bar because Senhor Nair had arrived. This was the signal for the merchants to take their morning break. They all came to the bar in spite of the morning's boycott because that was where Senhor Nair went first. There were more than ten men, and naturally they talked about the murder.

"Nobody from the police was here this morning," I said, realizing the fear of the police had kept them away.

Senhor Nair paid for the first round. That meant that seven rounds would follow because everyone except Mylorde and João would pay for a round.

"I wonder whether she was killed with Jussuf's gun or another weapon," mused the watchmaker.

"They will know this by now because I have given the captain the empty cartridge that Jussuf used in the morning. Do any of you know who had the gun at the end?"

"I won the last game," said Mylorde, "but the gun was gone when I wanted to pick it up from the counter. Did any of you see who took it?"

They looked at each other while they all shook their heads.

"Have they searched the room of the girl already?" asked Senhor Abraham.

"No," said the watchmaker who was her landlord. "but I have looked in. The room was quite dirty, but I don't think anybody was in the room since yesterday. I didn't touch anything, of course."

I tried to remember whether I had seen her key with the other things around the corpse, but I was sure there wasn't any. It lay probably under her doormat, as usual, but Senhor Carlos would have a spare key.

"Such a thing wouldn't have happened in Soviet Russia. They have little crime and no prostitution."

Senhor Abraham bored us all to death with his constant comparisons with Soviet Russia; it sounded like a broken gramophone record that repeated the same little fragment over and over.

"Donna Irma's reaction is that we should all be glad that we got rid of her. I am afraid the silly thing was jealous."

Senhor Abraham ordered the second round of drinks. They all went out and stood in the avenida, and I could no longer follow the conversation.

The bank president himself with two of his tellers came to the bar next. One of them asked his boss whether he could rent the apartment above the bank for his family. This was the apartment where Emilio and Chico lived. The president said that that would be fine; he could move in next week. He wanted to paint the place before he rented it again.

I had not known that the two intended to move out and wondered whether this had anything to do with yesterday's murder. Maybe they were on the verge of breaking up.

Quietly and without sirens the police car had driven up, and Captain Alfredo in an elegant uniform entered, followed by a sloppily dressed man in civilian dress.

"Do you know where the girl lived?" he asked the group in front of the bar.

"I was her landlord," said Senhor Carlos. "Do you want the key? I can't go with you because clients are coming to my shop."

He handed Captain Alfredo the key and hurried across the avenida where two ladies were waiting before his shop.

"Would you show me the place?" he asked me.

I had never been to Roberta's room, but I was very curious to see how the prostitute had lived; it might be a titillating experience, but I really couldn't leave the bar.

Senhor Nair came to my rescue. "Donna Anna Maria," he said, smiling because he had noticed my eagerness. "Don't worry. Go with him; I'll take care of the bar. I know the prices, and I have all the time in the world."

I gladly accepted his offer. I knew that I could trust him. He had taken care of the bar before to help me out.

I crossed the avenida with the captain, and we entered the passageway between Senhor Carlos' shop and the bank. The yard was without greenery. Only a basin for washing and a dirty cement floor.

"I guess Roberta's key is still under the doormat," I volunteered. "I didn't see it among her things."

"You are right, we did not find it. But it might have been in the missing wallet."

The key was under the doormat. Captain Alfredo remarked, "It seems that nobody was here."

I contradicted, "This means nothing. The thief of the wallet could have searched her room and left the key. You better look it over for fingerprints."

"Do you want to play detective?" the captain asked me with a smile. But he picked the key up with a clean handkerchief and put it in his pocket. Then he opened the door with Senhor Carlos' key.

The stench from spoiled food and rat drippings was overwhelming. We had to hold our noses.

First we came to a small entranceway that served as a kitchen. The chipped sink was full of dirty dishes. A small table beside the sink was covered with an old soiled oil cloth. On the table stood a dirty kerosene burner and two pots, one with rice and the other with cooked black beans. On the burner was a sooty tea kettle. A half-empty bottle of pinga stood next to the pots. Under the table was a garbage can and a kerosene canister. It was from the garbage that the odor emanated. Above the table were shelves that were filled with brown grocery bags that held sugar, rice, beans, salt and a few crusts of bread.

"She doesn't seem to have spent a lot of money for food," I remarked.

"She might have saved her money. I want to investigate the robbery angle of this case. It could have been armed robbery. But I am
not yet sure of it."

I had nothing against his theory. If he thought that the robber
was the murderer, he would leave us people in Alta Vista in peace and
look for his suspect elsewhere.

From the hallway we entered the room through a narrow door.
I still shuddered that the children and I had eaten food that was prepared in this filthy kitchen.

Senhor Alfredo closed the door behind us to escape the stench.

The room was about twelve by twelve feet. It had one large window to the court yard. Most of the room was occupied by a large
brass bed. It was unmade and smelled of unwashed humanity, but it
had clean looking mauve colored bed sheets and a quilt with a nice
pattern.

A small dresser with a partly blind mirror, a wash basin on a
stand, a table with a torn lace tablecloth, and two torn rattan chairs
were the only furniture. The room had no closet. Dresses and a robe
hung on pegs on the wall.

The walls were white-washed, but they had stains and fly specks.
Above the bed was an unframed poster with a picture of Nossa Senhora Apparecida.

"Nossa Senhora didn't lift a finger to help poor Roberta," I said
sarcastically.

"Don't blaspheme," answered the captain.

"I didn't intend to blaspheme," I replied. "I only stated a fact."

On the dresser were two framed photographs. One was Roberta
with a young man. It was quite faded. The other picture was new. It
was of little Innocencia. She wore a long, white dress with a veil and
held a large candle in her hand. The pretty first communicant had a
much lighter complexion than her mother. The man in the faded picture was probably her father.

On the table stood an empty bottle and one glass. In the table
drawer was costume jewelry and several boxes with condoms. Above
the table was a flyspecked calendar of last year with a picture of a
naked girl. On one of the chairs was another robe and the formless
sweater that she usually wore on cold days. The blood-spattered
blouse that she wore yesterday morning lay on the other chair.

"She must have lost some blood during her fight with Donna
Linda," remarked the captain as he fingered the blouse.

"Yes, they were really in each other's hair and face. When she
left the bar, Roberta held a strand of hair from the professora in her
hand. When you see the professora, you will probably see the scratches
that Roberta made. By the way, did you see any scratches on the
body?"

"Yes, she had lacerations on her neck and arms."

Suddenly the captain dived under the bed in spite of his immaculate uniform. He returned with Roberta's slippers and a gunny sack full of dirty laundry which explained why the drawers in the dresser were nearly empty. Captain Alfredo didn't examine the contents of the sack because they were so dirty and smelled so bad. But he took a brush from the top of the dresser to dust his uniform.

I felt sick to my stomach from the smell and from disappointment. I had expected to find a lover's nest, a little bit of luxury and romance, something titillating, maybe some pornography, but all we saw were smut and poverty. It was very depressing, and a wave of pity flooded over me. If I only could bring her back to life.

"I have to get my colleague to take fingerprints. Then we can compare them with your clientele, and we can eliminate a few suspects."

"Do you believe the murderer was one of her customers?"

"I can't tell at this stage, but we have to check out the alibis of her customers as well as the ones of the people who gambled for the gun. Thanks to your cooperation we know that the fatal shot was fired from Jussuf's gun or a gun with the same caliber. When we find the bullet that was shot in the morning, we can be sure."

"The bullet is probably somewhere in the street. It missed and ricocheted from the wall of the house. I, or your men should have looked for it."

As I mentioned before, the drawers in the dresser were nearly empty except for Innocencia's first communion dress which was folded carefully and wrapped in tissue paper. The dress reminded me of Roberta's golden cross.

"What did you do with the golden cross?" I asked.

"They took it off. I have it in my pocket. I think the child should have it."

"Are they going to put Innocencia in an orphanage?"

"That's none of my business. I have to solve the murder case. I guess she will stay with the foster parents for the time being."

"I think I will visit Innocencia," I said impulsively. It was a spur of the moment decision that surprised me after the words were out.

"That's a good idea," said the captain. "I don't have much confidence in our social workers. After the story that you told me yesterday night, I feel sorry for the little girl myself. It would be nice if the foster parents would adopt her."

"I think they looked after the girl because they needed the money. I will ask a friend of mine whether she knows of somebody who might adopt the child," I said, thinking of Donna Esmeralda.

"When you go to see the child, you could take the cross and the dress with you. I will arrange for you to get the things."

While we talked, we had come back to the bar. I invited the captain and his colleague for a cafezinho, and we continued to talk. Senhor Nair still stood behind the counter.

"I wanted to ask you another question, Donna Anna Maria," continued Captain Alfredo as he sipped the coffee. "I compared your testimony with the photos we have taken. You mentioned color crayons and candies that she had as presents for her daughter. I couldn't find them on the photos."

I wondered whether Sezinho could have been the culprit, but it was not in his nature to steal. Anyway, I would have to ask him before the captain got on his trail.

"I can prove my statement about the articles on the scene of the crime. Our friend Kurt took pictures of it long before the police arrived."

"Why did you not tell about this yesterday?"

"I had forgotten all about it. You remember how tired I was. Kurt left right away to develop his pictures. He wanted to sell them to the *Folhas.*"

The captain suppressed an expletive.

"I am sure Kurt will be here tonight to show us the pictures; if you stay long enough you may see them."

"You also talked about a wallet that we did not find."

"My husband saw the man who took it."

"Yes, he told us. He could get into trouble for this as an accessory after the fact."

"Willy can take care of himself," I said with more assurance than I felt.

Captain Alfredo sent the man who came with him and the driver of the squad car to Roberta's room to take fingerprints, then he asked me, "Where can I telephone from here?"

"The only telephone in the avenida is in the pharmacy. There is always a queue of people who want to use it."

"Then I better go to the police station for my call. *Aste logo,* goodbye," he said, and drove away.

Senhor Nair made two rabo de gallos, one for himself and one for me, after everybody had left. He paid for both of them. I did not want to accept the money because I wanted to show my gratitude to him for taking care of the bar, but I lost. He paid.

After a while Donna Aurora showed up with the children. The bambino, who had not seen me all day, ran into my arms and kissed me. I felt good and kissed Enrico and Angela, too. Angela was surprised and embarrassed. I did not kiss the children very often because I was afraid they would smell the pinga on my breath.

"Mama," said the confused Angela. "Don't do that in front of people."

She looked at Senhor Nair as if to ask for support. But he laughed and said, "I wish Donna Irma would kiss me like that."

Then he took the money he had taken in during my absence out of his pocket and gave it to me.

"The till was open for you. Why didn't you put it in?"

"I don't put my hands in somebody else's till." He said goodbye and left for his lunch and siesta.

Angela and Aurora told me about the house cleaning and washing of the morning while I prepared the left-overs from Sunday for our lunch.

Before we sat down, the candy vendor's pick-up appeared outside. I had to replenish our stock, and I was amazed how much I had to order. We must have sold much more than usual.

When I paid the man, I realized that the till was full of money from yesterday.

"Angela, you're going to have to eat without me. See that they all get enough to eat. I have to run to the bank before it closes."

I left some money for change and took the rest to the bank. It was full of people doing last minute business before closing time and I had to take my place in line. The two people in front of me talked about the murder. I listened, but they had not much to say that I didn't know myself. One new item, however, came up.

"Do you know that she kept her money in a stocking under her mattress?" I heard one of them say.

Aurora and Angela were still eating when I returned, but the two boys sat before their half-filled plates and only picked at their food.

"Why don't you eat?" I asked Enrico.

"I'm not hungry," he said peevishly.

"Are you sick?" I asked and tried to feel his forehead.

"Leave me alone," he said crossly. "I'm not sick. I'm just not hungry."

The bambino did not seem to be sick, but he also did not eat much. Both asked if they could be excused and I had to let them go.

Angela and Aurora stayed a little longer. We ate the left-over coffee cake and drank coffee. Of course we talked about the murder.

Aurora did not hear about the murder until she went out for the Sunday promenade in the avenida with her husband.

At that time the corpse had already been removed, and the avenida was full with Sunday strollers.

Aurora had heard the wildest stories about the murder, that the victim had been raped in the open street, that the girl had been tortured before the murder, that a great sum of money was missing, and other lurid details.

We still sat at the table when Captain Alfredo returned with four police officers in uniform.

"Good afternoon, Donna Maria," he greeted me with a handshake like a good friend.

"Good afternoon, Captain Alfredo," I said with equal friendliness. "Come have coffee with me."

He said something to the policemen who crossed the street to Roberta's place, and then sat down.

He took a piece of cake while I filled his cup.

"You know, we have found oodles of fingerprints in her room, mostly on the brass bed. There must have been as much traffic as in a railway station."

"Then she must have made a lot of money. How come she lived in such poverty?" I wondered. "The people in the bank said that she kept her money in a stocking under her mattress."

"This is only gossip?" he asked.

I nodded.

"But it is worth checking out." He left suddenly with the cake still on his plate and returned soon after with an empty nylon stocking in his hand.

"You were right, Donna Anna Maria, but the stocking was empty. Either the thief had come before us, or it was in the missing wallet."

The four cops came back to the bar. He called them in and asked me politely, "May we search the bar? We are looking for the murder weapon."

"Be my guest."

They looked behind the counter, in the refrigerator, behind the bottles on the shelves, in the display cases, they looked in every crate in the store room, but they could not find the gun. After they were convinced that it was not in the bar, they went outside to look in the street, in the yards and gardens that extended on both sides of the Rua Bonita.

Panthera Negra who had followed the men into the store room did not return. I went to get her, but she was nowhere to be found. Instead, I could hear the voices of the policemen who searched for the weapon in the orchard that bordered our storeroom. The murderer could have easily thrown the weapon over its low wall. The men shook the trees, but no gun fell out of the leaves.

The men stayed in and out of the bar all afternoon while I went about my business. They didn't disturb our patrons. Angela and Aurora had long gone home.

Wolfi returned around five. He had good news for me. He would be free on Wednesday afternoon. I would be able to go to the dentist.

Wolfi remained in the bar while I went to the pharmacy to call the dentist for an appointment. He would see me at three in the afternoon on Wednesday. From the pharmacy I went to our house. It was empty; the key was under the mat. The house was spotless, the clothes neatly ironed and sweet smelling. I put them away and cooked supper.

Willy came home at seven and so did the children. Wolfi was still at the bar. For once we sat down to a leisurely dinner at home.

Willy had the *Folhas*. We found only a short notice about the murder of a young woman in a back street of Vila Alta Vista. It said the police were investigating the murder which was connected with a robbery. Kurt's pictures were not in the paper.

Willy went back to the bar after supper and sent Wolfi home for his supper. Wolfi told us that he had talked with Kurt who had sold the pictures which had turned out very well.

We played Monopoly all evening and were in bed when Willy came home.

Bambino.

Chapter Four

TUESDAY, JUNE 22

Tuesday started as an ordinary routine day. The only difference from Monday was that the children came early to the bar for breakfast and that Mylorde did not show up at the usual time. When Senhor Nair returned from the city, he was surprised to find Mylorde's chair empty.

"Pusha Vida," he said, which is a very mild expletive. "This is the first time in many years that he didn't sit on this chair when I came home from work."

A short time after, all of Senhor Nair's friends collected for their morning drink and couldn't get over the fact that Mylorde was missing. But they changed the subject to talk about Roberta's missing money.

"I knew all the time about the money in the stocking," said Senhor Carlos without thinking.

"How could you know?" asked Senhor Abraham.

The watchmaker blushed, but did not reply.

'Could he also be one of her patrons?' I asked myself.

"Everybody who knew about the money will be investigated. You better keep your mouth shut about it when the police ask you. As for me, I have nothing to hide. I have never been in her house, and I didn't know about the money," said Senhor Abraham righteously.

"God knows how much it was," mused Toninho.

"You know," I joined the conversation, "I was in her room yesterday. I was appalled at the poverty in which she lived. They say her business was good. She spent a lot of money on booze, but she must have saved something besides paying for the child's upkeep."

"She spent a lot on booze," said Senhor Carlos.

"Not as much as you might think, unless she bought it somewhere else. I have a hunch that some of her customers brought their own bottles."

"You talk about her child. I didn't know she had a child," said Senhor Ernesto.

"Oh, yes," I replied. "She had a daughter with the very strange name of Innocencia. She lives with foster parents in the interior of the state. Roberta was a good mother. She was on her way to visit the child when she was shot."

"Have the foster parents been notified? What is going to happen to the child?" asked Senhor Nair.

"I really don't know," I said truthfully. "I have seen the picture of the girl. She is so pretty, it would be a pity if they had to send her to an orphanage."

Suddenly Sezinho stormed into the bar like a whirlwind. "Mylorde is dead!"

Before we could ask for details, he was out again to carry his message through town. We were all thunderstruck.

Yesterday he still sat on this chair and dispensed wisdom and advice. Today he was dead. It was not possible. But more children came by to announce the demise of the old man and to collect flowers for the burial. It was the custom to send flowers to the house of a death as soon as it was announced. Most people gave flowers from their gardens; some went to the florist.

Customers left to go to Mylorde's house to give him last honors. No time could be lost because people who died in the morning had to be buried the same day. People who died in the afternoon would be buried the next morning. Embalming was only for the very rich.

We experienced a number of deaths in our vicinity in Vila Alta Vista while we lived there. Each time I had the most disturbing nightmares when I imagined that the person was not really dead and woke up in the coffin and slowly died from suffocation. This fear was shared by many, and we heard horror stories of people who were exhumed with broken fingernails and scratches on the coffin lid, or stories about weird noises coming from fresh tombs.

The street was soon full of people running to Mylorde's house, but I could not go with them because I did not want to close the bar. Finally I decided to close the bar, when Angela showed up with a large bouquet of geraniums from our garden. They were the only flowers that bloomed all year round.

"That was nice of you to pick the flowers," I welcomed her. "But please, let me go first and stay here until I come back."

"No, Mama," she said firmly. "The flowers are mine. I picked them. I want to take them myself."

I shrugged my shoulders. "All right, but come back soon so that

I can go before they take him away."

Mylorde was old enough to die, and Donna Esmeralda was probably well provided for. His death was not tragic. Donna Esmeralda would keep busy with her foster children and her church work, and his friends would soon forget him.

While I waited for Angela's return, I received a shipment of beer and soft drinks. The men were very friendly and offered to take the crates to the store room and then take out the empty bottles. When they had finished, one of them told me:

"Donna Anna Maria, do you know that you have a hole in the wall of your store room that goes all the way to the outside?"

"Thanks for telling me. I suspected something because the cat has found a way from the bar to the garden. I must tell Willy to repair it."

I treated them all to pinga and joined them for a drink while I told them about the murder. They had already heard about it. After I paid the invoice, they left.

Angela came in out of breath. "Hurry Mama, the hearse has already come. I can stay here."

Mylorde still lay on his bed. He was not yet in the coffin. He looked very elegant in his Sunday best suit. His wrinkles were smoothed out of his waxen face. He looked younger than in life but very dead. I stood at the foot end of the bed and murmured a prayer for the repose of his soul.

He had suffered a stroke that morning. I prayed that his hands would not need to scratch the lids of the coffin.

"What a beautiful corpse," Donna Esmeralda repeated over and over. "What a beautiful corpse."

Most of the children of the neighborhood stood in the street to follow the hearse. They admired the beautiful, shining black horses and the old fashioned hearse of carved ebony wood. Two men in black unloaded the coffin which was very elaborate because Mylorde was wealthy and Donna Esmeralda wanted to show off.

My boys stood in a group together with the little Japanese boys. When the bambino saw me, he ran to me. "Mama, Mylorde has been shot."

"No," I spoke calmly. "Mylorde has not been shot. He was old and his days were full. God has called him to heaven."

"Did God call Roberta to heaven?"

"I don't know, but if he let her die, he must have had a reason for it."

We all stood in the street when they loaded the coffin on the

hearse. Most of the people followed the hearse to the end of Vila Alta
Vista, but I did not follow. Instead, I returned to the bar.

"If you run, you can still catch up with them," I told Angela.

As soon as she was out, I took a large draught of pinga right out
of the bottle, and then I poured myself a waterglass full with the
stuff.

The next two hours passed without incident. Many people came
to buy pinga in bottles to brew the traditional hot toddy made from
sugar, pinga, and ginger root that was a necessary feature of the celebration of the feast of São João, which coincided with the winter
solstice.

Senhor Abraham planned to have a party in his house that evening. The festivities went on during the whole month of June, culmi-
nating that week. Senhor Abraham had announced the first of our
block parties. Senhor Ernesto, surprisingly, had invited us for Wednesday night, and Donna Maria, Sezinho's mother, had planned a
party in the street for all the neighbors.

Sezinho passed by with a huge cookie sheet to go to the bakery.
The bakery baked its bread in the early morning and then again in
the afternoon. In between, the people of the community could use
the ovens for a small fee.

The children returned tired, hungry and elated from the funeral
procession. I don't know why funerals make a person so hungry, but
I was prepared for big appetites and had fried potatoes waiting for
them. This time, even Enrico and the bambino ate with gusto and
relish.

On my way back from Mylorde's house, I had collected pebbles
along the way, and before I sent Angela home, I went to the store
room and stuffed them in the hole as well as I could. Later, Willy
could pour cement over them.

The customers in the bar did not talk any more about the murder but about Mylorde's testament that would be read on Friday in
the notary's office. It was not a custom among simple people to make
a testament, and the fact that Mylorde had made a last will was the
cause of much conjecture.

Nobody knew about any relatives that Mylorde might have included in his will. We finally agreed that Mylorde must have illegiti-
mate children that he wanted to include in his testament.

The reappearance of Captain Alfredo with the fingerprint expert
reminded us again of the unsolved murder. The captain wanted to fingerprint everybody who was in the bar on Sunday morning.

He greeted me, "Donna Anna Maria," and he had a leery smile

on his face. "You won't believe this. The autopsy has shown that the girl was three months pregnant. It must have been on purpose, because we found enough condoms in her room and her purse for an army."

"Condoms don't always work," I said dryly.

"She also could have intended to trap one of her customers."

I was not sure whether the captain connected the murder with the pregnancy. It certainly gave a new twist to the question of motive. However, the captain had not given up the search for the money, in order to find the culprit.

Wolfi showed up soon after the captain. The captain asked me if they could take the fingerprints here in the bar to save the people the inconvenience of going to the police station. I agreed reluctantly. They set up their apparatus on one of the tables, and Wolfi was the first one to have his taken. After the expert compared his prints with the ones from Roberta's room, he said to me, "Donna Anna Maria, you can sleep in peace. Your son is cleared."

It was then that I realized that Wolfi was one of the prime suspects because he was at the murder scene, and nobody had seen him during the crucial time.

Wolfi washed his hands, and from then on acted as a messenger, calling the people whom the captain wanted to fingerprint. A number of kids stood in the street and watched the proceedings.

I wasn't too happy about the fingerprinting, because the people washed their hands afterwards in our wash room and trailed the black ink on the floor all over the bar. It would take Aurora a lot of elbow-grease to clean the place up again.

On the other hand, I was glad that the fingerprinting took place under my eyes because I was curious to know how the case and its solution took course.

Fingerprinting, and watching it, created a lot of thirst. So Angela and I had much to do. We had no time to supervise Enrico and the bambino who played somewhere outside in the dark.

When the police were done with all of the people in the bar and had fingerprinted Angela and myself, Captain Alfredo consulted his list and had the following names he still wanted: Willy, Francisco Almão, Jussuf, Donna Linda, Senhor Alberto, Emilio, Chico and Mylorde.

"You can't get Mylorde any more. He died this morning and is already buried."

"I hope you don't have to exhume him to fingerprint the old man," remarked Senhor Nair pompously.

"I don't think we need his prints. I guess I have to eliminate his name from the list of suspects."

Wolfi had been to Chico's house half an hour ago to call him and Emilio to the bar and was now on his way to Willy's cousin's house to tell his wife that he should come to the bar as soon as he came home.

Neither Chico nor Emilio had shown up. Captain Alfredo sent the driver of his car to fetch the two men. He returned after a short while without them.

"They were at home when I first sent for them," said the captain.

"Funny," said the driver. "I knocked at the door, but nobody answered. It was silent inside as if nobody were at home."

"I'll make out a search warrant, so you can break in, if nobody opens."

While he was writing the warrant, the Alta Vista squad car stopped in front of the bar to see whether Captain Alfredo needed help.

The captain sent them to fetch Donna Linda and Senhor Alberto. They returned presently with Sezinho, who wanted also to be finger-printed.

"My father was also in the bar on Sunday; he will come tonight when he comes home," said Sezinho, feeling very important. "But Senhor Alberto will not be in Alta Vista before next Thursday."

"Can't your sister get hold of him?" asked the captain impatient-ly.

"No, he is with his wife and children during the week."

"Where does he live?"

"He didn't tell us. He is afraid Apparecida would go to his wife and tell her about her baby," explained Sezinho, matter of factly.

"Why didn't you get Donna Linda," asked Captain Alfredo, turn-ing to the second policeman.

"She was not at home. A blind lady opened the door. She was very friendly and said that she would tell her sister to come to the bar as soon as she came home. But she didn't expect Donna Linda before tomorrow morning, because she went to a party in another part of town."

"We are also looking for a man by the name of Jussuf," said the fingerprint man.

"Oh, he wouldn't be here before Thursday evening. He is not in São Paulo during the week. Your best chance to meet him and Senhor Alberto is to come to our São João party on Thursday night. Everybody will be there," I said smiling. "May I invite you to our party, Captain Alfredo?"

"That's kind of you, Donna Anna Maria, but I will be off duty. We don't investigate murders on the feast of São João. We want to celebrate also, you know."

As the driver had not yet come back from Chico's place, the captain sent the two policemen also across the street. In the meantime, Wolfi returned out of breath.

Chico Almão will come later; he is not home yet," he said, full of importance.

"Have you talked with the other Chico, across the street, when you were over there?" asked the captain sternly.

"Sure thing," answered Wolfi. "Funny the way he behaved. He came out on the landing and shut the door behind him. He didn't let me come in."

"Chico and Emilio planned to move out already before the murder."

"Why didn't you tell me?"

"Why didn't you ask?" I snapped back. "Anyway this had nothing to do with the murder. Everybody knew they were homosexuals, and they were afraid the police were after them. You know, Janio Quadros and his vice squad."

"Mama," piped in Angela, "I wanted to ask you for a long time. What does that word mean, homosexual?"

I was embarrassed. The bystanders looked at me, eager to hear what I had to say.

"Oh, dear, I cannot tell you in front of all the people. Ask me at home, and I will explain it to you."

But Wolfi had no inhibitions. "That's simple," he lectured, "Homosexual means that a man has sexual relations with another man. Of course, no priest will marry them so they live in sin. Why they call it a crime, I do not know."

"Is it really a crime?" Angela asked, but nobody answered her.

We heard the professora panting from afar, long before she came in. Her face was purple when she staggered in. She must have been home dead drunk when her sister said that she was at a party.

She was boiling with rage. "You damned sons of bitches," she said. "You have no business to interrupt me, when I . . ." There she stopped herself. She became aware that she had sinned against her dignity as a teacher. She was also aware that Sezinho regarded her with terror-stricken eyes.

"You can go back to bed as soon as we have taken your fingerprints," said the captain with a smile. "We will interview you when you are sobered up."

After the prints were taken, she tottered to the john to wash her hands. She had to steady herself on the wall where she left prints of her inky hands. I followed with a rag to clean after her which enraged her even more.

"You drunken slattern," she shouted at me. "Don't you set yourself up as my judge. You aren't any better than I."

I had a strong impulse to hit her. But I managed to control myself and swallow my anger.

The two men who had gone to Chico's apartment returned empty-handed. They said that the apartment was empty.

"Wolfi," said Captain Alfredo in a stern voice, "you helped them to escape. You knew why they were in trouble. It is a crime to help and abet a criminal. I could arrest you for this."

"You incompetent nincompoop," my repressed anger erupted now. "You let out your disappointment on an innocent child!"

"Calma, calma, Donna Anna Maria," he laughed. "The mother protecting her brood. I was only joking."

"Look, policeman," I said, "instead of threatening little kids and law-abiding citizens, send your men over there and let them take fingerprints. Those two boys have at least left their fingerprints in their apartment, if nothing else.

"You have a point there," admitted Captain Alfredo.

"If you had the least bit of intelligence, you could have figured that out for yourself. What a country where morons like you lead murder investigations."

"Donna Anna Maria, you better watch your tongue. You are meddling too much with my work. Do I have to punish you for contempt for authority?"

"I'm sorry," I said, after I had regained my senses. "But what can a mother do when her children are attacked.

I filled two glasses with pinga and said docilely, "Let us make peace and drink to continued cooperation."

He accepted the pinga but did not reply.

Then he sent his men to the apartment to take fingerprints.

"Actually you have been quite helpful," he said at last. "But for God's sake, don't be so touchy. Your son is old enough to fend for himself. If you interfere too much with him, he'll resent you."

The people in the bar had followed my outburst with enthusiasm. They seemed ready to applaud me. They had never heard me use such strong language. But now, they left one by one to go home for supper.

Captain Alfredo sat down to write his report and Angela looked after her little brothers. Wolfi washed the dishes, and I cleaned up the mess of water and ink in the bar.

I watched the captain. If he wasn't a great intellectual light, he was at least extremely attractive with his fine profile and his gleaming white teeth, like an ad for toothpaste. Self consciously I slipped into the wash room, combed my hair and put on fresh lipstick.

When I got out, I stepped behind the counter to get a cup of coffee.

"Mama," rebuked Wolfi, "you shouldn't have gotten so mad at the captain. I knew he was only teasing. I had done nothing wrong. I told Chico the same way as I told the other people. How could I know that they were going to move out?"

"It was really my fault," I admitted. "I should have told the captain."

Suddenly Jussuf appeared in the doorway.

"What the heck are you doing here in the middle of the week?" I greeted him, not too politely.

Jussuf looked at me, quite puzzled. "No business this week. The people spend all their money for the feast of São João. It is a lot more fun here in São Paulo. I want to go to Senhor Abraham's party tonight."

"Don't forget our party on Thursday."

"Sure thing. I'll be there," he nodded. "Now give me a pinga and I'll treat you for one."

Then he looked around in the bar, noticed the captain, and asked me in a low voice, "Who is this type?"

"Don't you know that Roberta was shot last Sunday?" I replied. "This is Captain Alfredo from homicide."

"Roberta shot?" He was completely thrown off-balance by this news.

"Yes, we have had a lot of excitement since then. How come you didn't know?"

"Donna Anna Maria," he sighed, "I was completely drunk that day. I don't know how I got home. I woke up Monday morning in my room, fully dressed with my shoes on. I left Monday afternoon, but I came back today as I told you."

The captain had looked up and observed our chat. "Would you please introduce me to this gentleman?"

"This is our friend Jussuf Kattan who brought the gun to the bar last Sunday. Jussuf, this is Captain Alfredo from homicide."

"Glad to meet you," murmured the captain. "How do you do. Please wait until my men are back. We have to fingerprint you. We have fingerprinted all the people who were in the bar on Sunday morning. You are actually one of the suspects."

"One of the suspects? That's great. I didn't even know that somebody had been murdered."

"Were you in this bar on Sunday morning."

"Sure, I'm here every Sunday. I have a booth in the feira."

"Did you bring a revolver to this bar?"

"Sure enough. I lost it, too."

"Did you know the murdered girl?"

"Of course, everyone knew her. She was one of the best-known characters in this neighborhood."

"When did you leave?"

"I don't have the slightest idea."

"This young man," and he pointed at Wolfi, "has testified that you fell asleep in the bar after the rest of the customers had left, that he woke you up later, and that you left the bar shortly before the shot was fired, right after the Corinthians shot the second goal."

Jussuf looked thunderstruck. "I don't remember anything."

"Jussuf," I said, "don't answer. This is improper procedure to ask you here in front of us."

"You are right, as always, Donna Anna Maria," said the captain sarcastically. "Senhor Kattan, you will come with me to headquarters for questioning."

"Why should I go to the police?" said Jussuf indignantly. "I have done nothing wrong."

"Do you want me to ask you about your relations with the deceased in front of Donna Anna Maria?"

Jussuf blushed. The captain addressed his driver. "Have a look at him. We will take him with us when we leave."

Then Chico Almão showed up. I gave him a pinga and Jussuf told him, "Imagine, I am a murder suspect, and I didn't even know there was a murder."

"You were so damned drunk that you didn't know shit from shinola. But it is absolutely loco to fetch me. I went home with all the others and haven't been in this part of the town ever since."

"When did you hear about the crime?" asked the captain.

"When my daughter returned from her promenade in the avenida on Sunday evening."

They went to the other end of the bar where they talked with the captain. The men returned from Chico's apartment and took Chico's and Jussuf's fingerprints.

"Since you are already here," I told Chico Almão, "you may as well stay until Willy comes home. It must be any minute now."

Finally Willy arrived with Kurt. The captain had Willy and Kurt fingerprinted and then left with Jussuf and his men.

Kurt had a huge oven-fresh pizza with him to celebrate the sale of his pictures. Willy had also the last edition of the *Folhas*. Kurt's picture was not yet published, only a small article without a fat headline on one of the back pages told about the murder in Vila Alta Vista.

It said that the police were on the track of a suspect, that the murder was connected with the theft of a large sum of money which was in the missing wallet and that the murdered girl was a lady of ill repute.

I went home with Kurt while Willy stayed in the bar with his cousin.

The pizza feast at home was enjoyable as were all our visits with

Kurt. Afterwards, I returned to the bar to give Willy and his cousin their share of the pizza. I sat down with them to recount the many events of the day. Neither had heard of Mylorde's demise, although the poor man was already buried.

Then I told them about the fingerprinting and Chico and Emilio disappearing.

"I don't understand why they had to make me come all the way for the fingerprints; I had nothing to do with the murder," said Chico Almão.

"Damn it," grunted Willy, "why the fingerprints? I have never touched the dirty bitch or been in her stinking room."

"Kurt wasn't even here Sunday morning, and they got him, too," I remarked. "They just want to do a thorough job."

"Do you think that man near the corpse was really a reporter?" I continued, since nobody reacted to my former remark.

"I have my doubts now," said Willy pensively. "At that time I believed him. He looked authentic enough and I didn't know there was any money in the wallet."

"Did you tell the police about the mystery man?" asked his cousin.

"Of course. But I didn't say that he was a reporter. I didn't want to spoil his joke. Maybe I should tell them."

"They will only make trouble for you and accuse you of the theft," observed Chico.

"There must have been others who passed by. Not only Willy." My protective instinct asserted itself. "Anyway, the police know about the missing wallet. I told them and I also told about Kurt's pictures."

"Then they know that it wasn't an armed robbery," stated Chico.

"Maybe the mystery man shot her first and then came back for the money," mused Willy. "But it is not very plausible. I think he was a genuine reporter who wanted to put one over on the police."

"Did you know about the money?" I insisted.

"You silly goose," shouted Willy. "I told you already. How could I know. I had nothing to do with her."

Senhor Nair was our first evening customer. "What a shame about Mylorde," were his first words, and he reiterated all the details about how Donna Esmeralda had found the poor man on the floor of the toilet when she came home from church.

It seems that Mylorde was excited since Sunday and told his wife that he must change his testament, but that he didn't have a chance because his appointment with the notary was for Tuesday morning, when he was already dead.

While Senhor Nair rehashed the facts that I knew already, I left the bar to go home and change for the party. On my way down, I met

Senhor Abraham coming up to the bar.

"I'll see you later at the party."

"Thank you. I'd love to come to your fiesta, but we have a guest, Willy's assistant. May he come, too?"

"Sure, the more the merrier. Isn't he the one who made the beautiful pictures in your bar?"

"Yes, he's the one."

"Tell him that he is welcome. What about Willy?"

"I don't think so; he doesn't want to close the bar on an evening with so much business. It's a pity, because I enjoy a fiesta more when he is around."

I found it funny that a communist capitalist who was also a Jew should invite a woman from Nazi Germany to a fiesta in honor of a Catholic saint. But this was Brazil, the land of tolerance.

The children were happy that Kurt was coming to the fiesta, and Kurt was happy because he had never been to such a party, since it was his first year in Brazil. Besides, we were all looking forward to Donna Sarah's lavish food.

When we arrived at the party, the young people were already dancing in one of the rooms. Danny had a large collection of records, and my feet itched to join the dancing.

But after Wolfi and Kurt had dutifully danced each one dance with me, nobody invited me to dance, not because I was old and un-attractive, but because it was against the etiquette to invite a mar-ried woman to dance without permission of her husband, and my husband was not present to ask permission of. So, I had to sit with the older folks where I ate too much of Donna Sarah's delicacies.

Then it was time for the young people to light the bonfire. When it had burned down to embers, we fried churasco, holding the meat on large sticks in the fire; then we ate it with large slices of fresh bread.

The highlight of the fiesta was the launching of large paper bal-loons and the fireworks. Our balloons were large, larger than the law permitted. A torch was lit under the huge balloon made of tissue pa-per. The hot air filled the balloon until the air in the balloon was warmer than the surrounding air, and it slowly rose into the sky. The first balloons burned during the launching, but, at last, our balloon rose straight into the sky and floated away, accompanied by our wishes.

Then we had fireworks. While we sat around the fire and sang, balloons drifted by like giant moons in the sky.

Suddenly we heard the sirens of the fire brigade in the avenida. The movie theater had caught fire when a burning balloon fell on its roof. All the guests left to watch the fire.

I went into the bar to give Willy leftovers from the party and a cup of hot toddy. He had no customers.

Willy wanted to wait for the firewatchers to come back, but I convinced him to call it a day and go home. We went to bed and didn't hear the children come home.

Avenida Tucuruvi.

Chapter Five

WEDNESDAY, JUNE 23

Panthera Negra was not in front of the house when I left home on Wednesday morning. First I thought it was because of the fog that shrouded São Paulo, but then I realized that she was probably trapped in the bar since I had closed her exit.

Yesterday had been a clear, star-studded night, but now the weather had changed. I had felt the change of weather because I suffered an attack of asthma during the night. Normally, my asthma improved during winter, the dry season, but a change of weather was bad for me. I had to get up in the middle of the night to take medicine. Then I had to sit in an armchair and play solitaire until the medicine took effect, and I could cough up and go back to sleep.

Now I was tired and depressed and I missed the friendly presence of the cat that usually rubbed affectionately on my legs.

The steep ascent to the bar increased my breathing difficulties. Panthera mewed miserably in the bar. I let her out and poured milk for her in a saucer.

I ate breakfast alone because Willy had left earlier while I was still in bed. He had to go on a two-day inspection to measure the progress of the new generator in Cubatão that was under construction.

Sometimes a hot drink prevented an attack of asthma, but this time it did not pass, and I had forgotten the medicine at home.

At least I did not have to clean up the bar because I was expecting Aurora who came Wednesday this week instead of Thursday because of the feast of St. John.

I didn't make ice cream because I was too tired and because of bad weather. All I could do was to pour myself a drink of pinga which made me even drowsier. I put my head on the cold marble of the table and felt sorry for myself.

I dozed off and dreamed about sun and warmth, but a monster chased me towards an abyss and made a big noise. The noise finally woke me up. It was the siren of a fire truck. "Another fire," I thought. But it was only the last engine that returned from the fire in the movie theatre.

I got up to take a chocolate bar from the display case. I couldn't believe my eyes. The large store of candy that I had bought on Monday was nearly gone. I was positively sure that we had not sold very much. Somebody must have stolen candy from it. Now I had to play detective in order to find the thief of the candy.

My first thought was about Sezinho. I had already suspected him of the theft of the color crayons and candy, and now he seemed to have also taken candy from the bar. Of course I had no proof, except that I had seen him near the corpse and that he was in and out of the bar at all times. I would have to question him.

Meanwhile, customers entered to buy breakfast items. Our profit on such things was negligible. But the former owner had sold them, and the people were accustomed to buy them from us. Besides, the same people bought also other things from our bar on which we made a higher profit.

Donna Maria was a faithful customer of low profit items, and she bought on credit, but she bought also bottled drinks. But neither she nor her daughter Apparecida came ever to the bar to eat or drink.

Donna Maria was a mulatto, but she had no idea where her white heritage came from, probably from one of the overseers on the plantation where her forefathers were slaves. Donna Maria's husband was pitch black, and of their two children, Sezinho was dark and Apparecida was light-skinned.

Apparecida was slim and lithe, and she had a sweet face with full lips, a small nose, large, liquid eyes and a velvety, glowing golden complexion. Her hair was long and smooth, her hands were small and delicate and she didn't want to ruin them with hard work. She had lived with Senhor Alberto for more than three years.

She met Senhor Alberto in the feira, where he had a novelty booth. They loved each other dearly, but Senhor Alberto could not get rid of his Polish wife because there was no divorce in Brazil. He provided generously for Apparecida and their golden haired baby.

The baby was a doll with his strange coloring, his round eyes and thick, kinky hair. He was very fat and smiled happily to everyone passing in front of the house where he usually sat on the terrace in his pen. Apparecida was sitting in a rocker beside him with her hands folded over her swelling belly or with mending or embroidery in her hands.

Donna Maria stood day in, day out behind the washing trough. She did the washing for the bachelors in the neighborhood, like Jussuf, Chico and Emilio. She expected no help from her pretty daughter and was satisfied when Apparecida volunteered to iron or to mend.

Donna Aurora came at nine and mopped the bar and removed the last traces of the fingerprint mess. Then she went to our house to wax and buff the floors.

I had the radio going and was listening to Senhor Nair's program. He was impersonal and played records that did not turn me on. Afterwards, another disk jockey took over, and I turned off the radio.

The children came to the bar to get money for tissue paper to make more balloons. At last Wolfi came. He was for once able to sleep as long as he wished. He relieved me; I went home and found Aurora in the middle of house-cleaning.

Angela said that she did not want to go to town with me because Donna Esmeralda had asked her to babysit for little Carmen while she went to the cemetery.

I called Enrico and the bambino to tell them that I would take them with me to the *cidade*.

"No," said Enrico to my surprise. "I want to stay home and play with my friends."

"That's strange," I said. "You usually jump at the idea of going to town. I have planned such a nice program for the afternoon."

Enrico seemed to struggle with himself. Finally he said without much enthusiasm, "Okay, Mama, I'll go with you."

The bambino echoed with the same lack of enthusiasm, "Okay, Mama, I'll go."

Normally they liked nothing better than to explore São Paulo with me.

There was nothing for me to do at home, so I returned to the bar. Wolfi was glad to have some free time because he, also, wanted to make a balloon.

"Mama," he said, "Senhor Ernesto invited all of us to his fiesta tonight. Can we go?"

"You and the children may go, but Papa is in Cubatão, and I have to stay in the bar."

Senhor Nair came in and asked me whether I had heard his German record on Monday.

"I completely forgot to thank you for it," I said warmly. "It really cheered me up. I was so depressed on Monday. Do it more often, please."

Senhor Abraham came in for his morning beer. I told him how much I had liked his fiesta, and then I added, "but I would have liked to dance a little. It's ridiculous that nobody asks a married woman to dance when her husband isn't present."

"Donna Anna Maria, you don't understand. We have to protect our ladies, even if they don't like it," explained Senhor Nair.

"You hypocrites with your double standards. Most of you run around with other women, but you demand that your wives remain faithful to you."

"But Donna Anna Maria, women are different from men."

"In Soviet Russia," this was of course Senhor Abraham, "there is divorce if two people cannot live together in peace. But here is no divorce. That is why so many men are unfaithful."

"What the heck is a woman to do when her husband does not satisfy her?" I flew off my handle again. "Is she supposed to be quiet, and suffer in silence and chastity?"

"Donna Anna Maria, how can you compare a man who goes out to his work every day with a woman who has to look after a household and children?"

"So what? Isn't a man also a father who should be a model to his children?"

"As for me, I am glad that I can count on Donna Irma to be at home when I get there."

"And you, you think you can do as you well please?"

I have never seen Senhor Nair get angry, but now he shouted, "That is none of your damn business, what I do. None of us runs as often to the cidade as you do."

"You better check on your own wife. I can well look after myself."

I was roaring mad because they gossiped already about my innocent excursions to the cidade with my children. I nearly told him about Donna Irma's plan to take a lover in order to get pregnant, but I was able to keep my mouth shut.

My customers paid and left. I thought that I had ruined our business for good, but I couldn't care less. I wanted to get rid of the bar anyway.

But after a while Senhor Nair and Senhor Abraham came back. "Let's forget the quarrel; after all, you are a German and have been brought up differently from us," said Senhor Nair.

I fixed them drinks and said, "This is on the house as a peace offering."

When Captain Alfredo showed up around noon, the bar was full of patrons.

"Hello, Captain Alfredo," said Senhor Nair cordially. "I read in the paper that you have a suspect."

"Yes and no," said the captain. "We don't have enough evidence. But the Arab knew that she had money, and we found his fingerprints in her room."

"Are you talking about Jussuf?" asked the watchmaker. "I also knew that she had money. That doesn't make me a suspect."

"The trouble is that most of you could have murdered her. You can't imagine how many matching fingerprints we have found. That filthy room was like a beehive."

I regarded my honorable clientele with amusement, they who

were so worried about the chastity of their wives. How many of
them had enjoyed themselves in the huge brass bed? I was glad that
Willy was none of them.

"But it was the Arab who brought the gun."

"Forget about it," interrupted Senhor Moses. "He lost it during
the game."

"He might have arranged the game to share suspicion with the
others. Nobody knows who had the gun last."

"No, Jussuf is not so smart," stated Senhor Abraham. "It was
Mylorde who started the game."

"I don't think any of you is a murderer. By the way Donna Anna
Maria, you gave me the clue that helped me to identify the gun as the
murder weapon."

"Because I gave you the cartridge?"

"No, because you told us to look for the bullet that was shot
in the morning. We found it in the dust. It was fired from the same
gun as the bullet in the girl."

That shut me up. After a while the captain continued. "Most
of you people have alibis for the time of the murder. Only about the
Arab we know definitely that he was in the street."

I tried to figure out why he talked so freely with us. Shouldn't
he keep the information to himself? Did he want to elicit more information from us? I decided that he would not get any information
about Jussuf from me.

"Have you found the whereabouts of Chico and Emilio?" Senhor Carlos changed the subject. I guess he felt the same way as I.

"No, but believe it or not, we have found prints from both of
them in the room of the prostitute."

"I'll be darned," I said. "That's strange."

We all thought that they were a gay couple. Emilio might have
been heterosexual. Could it be that Chico was jealous? He looked so
desperate when he, so unexpectedly, joined in the gambling.

"I would like to ask you a favor, Donna Anna Maria," said the
captain. "Could I interview a couple of people here, or would you
prefer that we go to the police station?"

"If you want to sit in the store room, that's alright. But not
here in the bar."

He called the cops in the car outside. They put again a table and
chairs in the store room. Then he sent his men to fetch his witnesses.

The first who showed up was Danny. I wondered whether he
also had left fingerprints on the brass bed. He wouldn't be the murderer, but Senhor Abraham in the role as an avenging father was plausible. But if the police were looking for a thief, neither father nor son
would qualify. I was even more surprised when Senhor Ernesto entered with a policeman. I could not imagine him in the role of an
avenging father. He would have cherished nothing more than that his

son showed any interest whatsoever in a female, even if it was a
whore.

He himself was too senile and decrepit to qualify as Roberta's
customer. In my vivid imagination I saw him arranging an appointment for his lackadaisical son.

I had to leave as Wolfi and the children arrived although I was
curious to know who the suspects were that Captain Alfredo wanted
to interrogate.

We took the bus to town and were soon finished at the dentist.
I went with the boys to several of our favorite haunts and went shopping.

Not much time was left, but I had promised the boys a treat,
and we went to a cafe.

So it was after five-thirty when we arrived at the bus terminal.
A large queue was in front of us when we took our places. The large
Praca de Correio, the Post Office Square, was black with people because most busses to the northwestern suburbs of São Paulo started
from here.

We were still far from the rainshelter when black clouds began to
cover the sky. A cold wind blew, and soon the first drops of a cloud-
burst began to fall.

We had warm wraps with us but were not prepared for one of
the rare rainshowers during winter time and had no umbrellas. When
we finally reached the sheltered area we were soaked to the skin and
had to wait another twenty minutes in the chilly wind.

In the bus it was warm and steamy. The chattering of the teeth
of the passangers competed with the loud rattling of the bus. My
asthmatic wheezing was a falsetto above the noise. It took thirty
agonizing minutes, standing in the tightly-packed steaming mass, to
get home.

"Mama, have you seen the *Folhas* tonight?" were Wolfi's first
words.

"Later, Wolfi," I gasped. "I have asthma. Sorry, you have to wait
until I come back."

"Take it easy, I can wait."

We were all three of us shivering and had to change from head to
toe. Fortunately, Angela had hot soup ready for us. She proudly
showed me the money she had earned and asked me whether she
could go to Senhor Ernesto's fiesta.

"You have to take the boys with you. Don't stay too late. I'll
tell Wolfi to send you home at eleven."

I took my medicine, and after it took effect I returned to the
bar, not because I was so eager to work, but because I felt the need
for a drink, and I didn't want to imbibe in front of the children.

I dressed as warm as I could and took the medicine along. I
hoped that I would not need it because a large dose of pinga some-

times helped as well. I also took a book along because I did not expect many customers.

The same as they wouldn't dance with me, they would not loiter
in the bar when I stood behind the counter at night instead of Willy.

I heard the crackling of fireworks from all directions. The steep
ascent made me cough and wheeze again, and it took a few minutes
until I could even talk.

Wolfi was grateful that I returned so soon. I told him to go
home and eat Angela's hot soup. But he said he didn't want to spoil
his appetite before the party.

I wanted him out of the bar as soon as possible, but I had to
ask him about the *Folhas.*

"Mama, Kurt's pictures are in it, and a long article. You must
read it yourself. Imagine, the man Papa saw was really a reporter."

At last Wolfi was gone, and I could finally take that much-
needed pinga. I sat down at a table with my glass and took the paper.
Right on the front page was Kurt's picture of the scene of the murder.
It was well-focused, all the articles that lay around in the street could
be well identified. The body was surrounded by a dark puddle, and
she had her hands covering her face, as if she wanted to protect herself.

On the first page, in thick print, was also the double headline:

IT WAS NOT ARMED ROBBERY
The Efficient Homicide Division of the Police of our Capital

I could speak Portuguese better than I could read it, and I didn't
have a dictionary with me in the bar, but I could more or less understand the content of the article.

It said that the picture was taken shortly after the murder by a
passing amateur photographer, long before the arrival of the police.
One of the *Folha*'s reporters also passed by chance through the avenida when something dark on the pavement in a side street attracted
his attention.

He stopped to investigate and saw a lonely corpse in the middle
of the street without any living soul in sight. He hid in a doorway
when he heard the sirens of the squad car.

The policemen entered a bar at the corner. Then they came out
and inspected the corpse in a cursory manner and then left to disperse
a crowd of children that tramped down the avenida. Again, the
corpse was left unguarded. A man came up the hill and stopped in
front of the corpse without any sign of shock or surprise at seeing a
corpse in the middle of the street.

Our reporter came out of hiding, identified himself to the man
as a reporter of the *Folhas.* He asked the man to witness as he took
the wallet of the deceased woman. He found out only later that the

wallet contained a considerable sum of money. Wallet and money had been handed over to the police this afternoon.

When the reporter saw the picture that the amateur photographer took, he noticed the color crayons and candy in it that were not there when he made his find.

We cannot publish the name of our reporter because he committed an unlawful act when he took the wallet, but we publish his story to point out the ineptitude of our police.

I was kind of relieved that the money, that belonged now to Innocencia, had been found. Furthermore, I was glad to have something to back me up when I accused Sezinho of the theft, as I intended to do. But that had to wait for tomorrow because Sezinho, like all the other children, was at Senhor Ernesto's fiesta.

The street was dark and deserted, and I felt forlorn and miserable. I changed from pinga to brandy because this is supposed to be better against a cold. Unexpectedly, the Professora tramped in to buy a couple of bottles of pinga. She did not seem to remember our recent spat and was sweet and friendly.

I offered her a shot of brandy and said, "Please, sit down and keep me company for a while; I feel so miserable and lonely tonight."

She sat down and accepted the brandy. "Why are you here tonight? Where is Senhor?"

"He is on an inspection tour in Cubatão and told me to keep the bar open. But I really shouldn't; I just had a bad attack of asthma and can barely stand up, weak as I am."

"I don't have much time because I am expecting company, but can you tell me why Sezinho acts so strangely?"

"Yes, something bothers the little boy since the murder."

"You are right. It began with the murder."

"Do you remember the fight you had with Roberta the morning before the murder?"

"What fight? I don't remember."

"Before you gambled for the gun. Your whole face was scratched and she tore out some of your hair."

"I remember the scratches and the headache. But I had no idea how I got them."

"You and Roberta stood here in the bar and cussed each other. Suddenly you were in each other's hair. Here in the hallway between the john and the store room."

"The whore and I? That's impossible!"

"Yes, we all, including Sezinho, watched the fight. Afterwards Roberta left, and you stayed to gamble for the gun."

"Gun? What gun?"

"The gun with which Roberta was shot."

Donna Linda looked at me with wide-open eyes. It was obvious that her surprise was genuine.

"I saw the gun twice in your hand. Didn't Captain Alfredo question you?"

"He took my fingerprints yesterday and sent for me this afternoon. But I was not at home."

"Didn't he interrogate your sister?"

"No, only the policeman who came to fetch me asked some questions."

"What did she tell him?"

"That I was in bed all Sunday afternoon, and that's the honest truth."

"Sezinho thinks that you have shot Roberta."

"Pusha vida," exclaimed the Professora. "The poor dear. That's what's bothering him."

"Say, have you ever been to Roberta's room?"

"What a question. Why should I? I had nothing to do with that bitch. Of course not."

"That's good. Captain Alfredo is after the people who left fingerprints in her room."

I had again a severe coughing spell.

"You should close the bar and go to bed, Donna Anna Maria. Let's go together. I have to leave also."

I agreed, and Donna Linda helped me with the shutters.

The children were not yet home. I took more medicine and fell asleep right away. When I awoke later with cough and asthma, the children slept peacefully in their beds.

The home of Annemarie and family.

Chapter Six

THURSDAY, JUNE 24

It was not only asthma but a beginning bronchitis that kept me awake last night. The room was cold, and I suffered from self-pity on top of everything else because Willy was not home. I brewed myself a hot toddy and finally fell into an exhausted sleep.

When the alarm clock went off, I turned it off without thinking and went back to sleep. Wolfi finally woke me up. He was mad because I let him oversleep, and he would be late for his work. I got up right away and was ready to leave before he had finished shaving his scant beard.

The steep hill seemed to be steeper than usual. Sezinho, with Panthera on his arm, waited in front of the shutter. I panted for breath, then I said, "Sezinho, please help me with the shutters and come in. I want to talk with you."

He opened the shutters, but he said, "I am busy right now, but I will come later."

He bought Senhor Alberto's favorite cigarettes, which reminded me of the fiesta tonight.

After he left, I gave Panthera her milk and sat down for a cup of coffee. I was too miserable to clean up or to make ice cream.

"I thought you were in the bar yesterday night. How did you get out?" I asked Panthera.

She regarded me with round eyes, rubbed herself against my legs, and sat on one of the chairs, purring loudly.

"Is the hole open again?" I asked her. She said nothing, only purred louder.

"Oh, you dumb creature. Now I have to get up and look for myself."

True enough. The cat had pushed the pebbles outside, and the hole was open again. It was really my fault. The pebbles would not hold without cement. However, I put them carefully back to close the hole.

The freshly shaved Wolfi came soon, and we breakfasted together. When I asked him about the party, he shrugged his shoulders. "So-so."

"Is that all?"

"You know, Mama, Angela is such a silly goose. All evening she and Danny held hands. She is only twelve, and Danny is nearly grown up. It is disgusting how she runs after older men."

"Actually, I don't worry too much; she is a very level-headed young lady."

"That's what you think. You should listen to her when she gabs with her girlfriends. Nothing but boys."

"That's natural for her age. By the way, what do you talk about with your boyfriends?"

"That's different. After all, we are boys, and much older."

"Even at your tender age you are poisoned by the double standard in this country. To change the subject, I have read the article in the *Folhas.* My suspicion is that Sezinho took the crayons and the candy. I also think that he has stolen candy from the bar."

Wolfi's reaction was unexpected. He blushed and said very positively, "No, it is not Sezinho who takes candy from the bar."

"Then you know who took them?"

"Yes, but I cannot tell you who it is."

"That's silly. Come, tell me."

"No, I gave my word not to tell you. It will not happen again."

Wolfi stood up and left although no bus was coming down the avenida.

Sezinho returned and asked, "What can I do for you, Donna Anna Maria?"

"No, Sezinho, I don't have an errand for you. I wanted to show you something."

I showed him the picture in the *Folhas,* and he looked at it with great interest.

"Is this the way you saw it?" I asked him.

He looked again very attentively. Then he pointed to the candy and crayons. "I didn't see that."

"You are right, they were not there when the police came. Look also at her hands. She clutches them over her face. They were open when the police saw the corpse."

"I didn't do it. I didn't do it."

"Sezinho, I don't accuse you of anything. What did you not do?"

"I didn't see any candy or crayons when I saw Roberta. I didn't take anything. I am not a thief."

"Don't lie to me. I saw you bend down. You didn't see me. I looked back just before I went around the corner. No need to protest. I will tell Captain Alfredo, and he will put you in prison."

"Don't do it, don't send me to prison! I am innocent."

It was like the eruption of a volcano. All his sufferings during the last days came to the surface. Finally he sobbed, "The Professora, the poor Professora."

"What the heck has the Professora to do with all this?"

Sezinho calmed down, and after a while he said, "The Professora killed Roberta. I know it. I must protect her. The poor Professora."

"Donna Linda? Are you crazy?" I was stupefied. "Donna Linda was at home and slept while somebody murdered Roberta."

"I can't believe it."

"Donna Linda was so drunk she couldn't have shot straight."

"The Professora can do a lot of things when she is drunk. She can even teach school, and the children don't notice."

"Don't worry about Donna Linda. Her sister will testify that she was at home."

"Donna Linda's sister is blind and alcoholic. She doesn't know what she says. I know that it was the Professora, and I had to protect her."

"How did you protect Donna Linda?"

"You know, Roberta had long black hair under her fingernails. Hair from Donna Linda. That's what I did. I took the hair out of Roberta's hand. It was terrible. The hands were cold and stiff. I couldn't put them back as they were before."

"Holy Mother of God! Of course they were Donna Linda's hairs. She pulled them out here in the bar. Roberta probably never washed her hands before leaving."

Sezinho looked at me with a glimmer of hope in his round eyes. "Do you really believe it was not the Professora?"

"Sezinho, I am positively sure, and so is Captain Alfredo."

"Then I didn't really protect her?" This new realization made him look suddenly crestfallen.

"I think you did help her in a way. She would have had a lot of troubles because of the hair in Roberta's hand."

Sezinho wiped his face with his dirty hands and smeared dirt all over his face."

"Now, go and wash your face," I said soothingly. "Do you want me to tell Donna Linda how you tried to protect her?"

"No, don't tell her. I am ashamed that I suspected her. She is much too good to do such a thing."

"I knew all the time that you suspected the Professora, and I told her so when she asked why you don't visit her any more. She likes you very much and will not be angry with you. She will be proud that you wanted to help her."

Sezinho sighed and went to the wash room. But I was not yet through with him.

When he returned with a shiny face, I continued, "But now, be honest with me. Why did you take the crayons and the candy?"

"Donna Anna Maria, I told you already, I never take anything. I am not a thief."

"Somebody must have taken them. It was for sure the same person who steals from the bar."

Sezinho was startled. "You know that somebody takes candy from the bar?"

"Yes, probably the same person."

"No, it was not the same person. He was at the movies."

"How do you know? Do you know the thief?"

He nodded.

"Who is it? Tell me."

"I gave my word of honor not to tell."

That sounded familiar. They were the same words that Wolfi had used.

"If you don't tell me, I'll go to Captain Alfredo and tell him that you removed the hair from the fingernails."

Sezinho cried again. Stonily, I continued, "and I will also tell him about the missing candy in the bar."

"Don't do that. You will be sorry," sobbed the little boy.

"But I have to report the theft to the police."

"It is Enrico. He took the candy."

"What do you say? That's not true!"

Sezinho cried again as I shouted at him. "Don't tell Enrico. I gave my word of honor not to tell."

"Shut up. Tell me what you know." I was so upset that I continued to shout at the poor Sezinho.

"He is going to beat me up."

"I promise you I will not tell, but tell me what you know." I finally forced myself to be calm.

"Donna Anna Maria, go see for yourself. The candy wrappers are under the house."

I was speechless. Sezinho seized the opportunity to run away. I was ready to cry with despair, but customers came to the bar and had to be served.

When Angela finally arrived, I did not say, "Good morning." Instead I asked her angrily, "Is it true that you flirted with Danny yesterday at the party?"

She blushed and nodded.

My hand shot out, and I hit her hard in the face. All my fingers were etched out in red. She looked at me, terrorstricken. Her eyes filled with tears, but she did not utter a word.

"We will talk about this later. Now I have to go home. You stay here."

"But Mama . . ."

"No Mama, please. I have to go."

I ran down the hill. Of course, I panted and wheezed when I got there. I did not enter the house but crawled under the house into the children's hide-out. The two boys were still in bed. Hundreds of empty candy wrappers lay on the floor. Here was the solution of the mystery of the missing candy.

My own son was the thief. I could not think rationally. I saw everything overblown to grotesque dimensions. First my rage turned against Enrico. I could have beaten him green and blue. I would have liked to scream. But instead, I absentmindedly grabbed a left-over candy bar and ate it. Then I lay down on the floor and cried bitterly.

I could not indulge for long in self pity because I began to cough and gasp for breath. I had to go to the house to take medicine.

I took the medicine. Then I filled a waterglass with pinga. Then I went to the washroom. I saw my swollen face in the mirror. I was disgusted with what I saw. I returned to the kitchen and took the glass with the pinga and poured it down the drain. Then I washed my face, went to bed, and fell into a deep sleep.

Angela woke me up an hour later. "Mama, what is the matter? Are you sick?"

"I think I am sick. I must have caught a cold yesterday in the rain."

"I was worried about you when you didn't come back. I left the bar when Senhor Nair came in."

"That's all right." I sat up in bed. My head hurt and burned like fire.

"Angela, did you know that Enrico stole from the bar?"

"Of course, Mama. We told him all the time to stop it, but we didn't want to tell you."

"Sit down and tell me what happened."

Angela sat down on the bed and told me a long story.

Shortly after we moved to the Rua Promirim, Enrico had troubles making friends with the children in the street. Nelson, a fat boy in our block, told the other children that he would beat them up if they played with the new German boy. He always called Enrico "Hun" and threatened to beat him up. As soon as Enrico left the house, the children would shout, "Little Hun, Nelson is going to beat you up."

Enrico was afraid to go to school and never left the house after he came home from school. His only friend was Walther, one of the greengrocer's sons. But neither he nor Walther were very strong, and they were both afraid of the gang of children.

Finally, Enrico started to take candy from the bar to bribe the children to leave him in peace. Soon they all knew that Enrico had his pockets always full with sweets.

He sent a message to Nelson that he would give him candy if he came to his house to play. So it happened that the place under our house became the center for the children.

Enrico had to take more and more candy to satisfy the demands of his playmates. But he was now the most popular boy in the block.

"And you knew this all the time?" I asked at last. "And you never told me?"

"He wouldn't let us. He was afraid you'd beat him up."

"Then why didn't you tell Papa?"

"Mama, you know we scarcely see him at all, and never without you being around."

"Angela, do you think we should sell the bar, and I should stay at home again?"

Her face lit up like the rising sun. "That would be wonderful. We would be a family again and do things together."

"I am going to talk with Papa. We must get rid of the bar. You have to help me today. I am too sick to work. But I will try to be there with you."

"I don't mind. Only get well again."

"And now, don't be afraid; tell me about you and Danny."

"There is nothing to tell. I know that I am too young to date. But he is such a nice boy. I really like to talk with him."

"After we sell the bar, when I am home again, you will be able to invite young people to our house. Only please, do nothing behind my back. Let's be friends and honest with each other."

"I am sorry I made you so mad."

"I am sorry too. I really should not have lost my temper, but I was so upset about Enrico, and you came in first and got all my anger."

"Don't hit Enrico. He will get mad at you."

Now we both laughed, and Angela said, "Mama, I love you," and hugged me.

I hugged her too and was glad that I had poured the pinga down the drain. I felt unworthy of Angela's love because I was suddenly ashamed that I was an alcoholic.

Angela said that the boys had their breakfast in the bar while I slept and that they were now playing with the Japanese boys in the greengrocery.

I sent Angela to the bar and followed shortly thereafter. Senhor Nair looked at me, and said, "Donna Anna Maria, you really look sick. I hope it is nothing serious."

"I caught a cold. Angela will do the work. I will just sit in a chair and do nothing. I only hope that Willy will be home soon."

"You should sell this place," said the watchmaker.

"You are perfectly right. We will sell the bar."

"The trouble is that Senhor Willy doesn't want to sell," continued Senhor Carlos. "He had some very reasonable offers, but they were not good enough for him and this precious place."

"He is definitely going to sell," I said with more conviction than

I felt. I wondered whether it was true, what the watchmaker said, and what Wolfi had said before.

Toninho, Walther's father, was also in the bar, and I asked him to send Enrico to me as soon as he got back.

He left soon, but neither Enrico nor the Bambino showed up in the bar.

Captain Alfredo showed up around noon.He seemed to be dejected. This was not surprising, after yesterday's article in the *Folhas*. I remembered that he said the other day he would take the feast day off, but now he had to work because of the new twist of the case. He said only "Hello," and went to Roberta's room.

Angela mixed drinks like an experienced bar maid. When the truck with beer and bottled drinks arrived, Captain Alfredo's driver helped Angela to take care of the crates.

The Bambino showed up for lunch, but he said he didn't know where Enrico was. He and Angela ate, but I had no appetite. Afterwards they left together to look for Enrico. I was alone in the bar when Donna Linda came in.

"Thanks a lot, Donna Maria. Sezinho and I had a good talk. He was ashamed that he suspected me of the murder."

"Does he believe now in your innocence?"

"I hope so. I hated the whore with all my heart, but I never would have killed her. Not even when I was under the influence of alcohol. You see, I am a very devout person. My religion is against violence."

"I always wondered about your religion; I was told that you are a member of the Macumba cult, and people say terrible things about it."

"It is a cult in which Christian and pagan elements are united. The African cults of the negro slaves and the native Indian religions of the jungles are really very meaningful."

"Why are your meetings so noisy?"

"Very simple, because we have drums and tom-toms instead of your Christian organs."

"And your loud chants replace the Christian hymns?"

"You got the idea. But, you know, we are ethical people who believe in god, Jesus and the Holy Virgin."

"What about witchcraft?"

"Ours is a secret sect. I cannot tell you about it. But be assured that we use only white magic. We use it only for good causes."

"Is macumba the same as voodoo?"

"Only in the way that it is based on practices of the African jungles. We have added more Indian and Christian motives to it."

It was the first time that Donna Linda spoke about her religion. "How come you belong to them?" I asked her.

"Because I am a negro, or rather a part negro."

It had never occurred to me that Donna Linda with her olive complexion and long straight hair was a negro. I thought she was of Mediterranean origin.

"I never talk about my origin. Let people believe what they want. I don't go around like that black hussy and proclaim that I am 'Portuguesa.' My mother was Portuguese, my father a light-skinned very handsome mestizo. A mixture of white, Indian and negro. You have never seen my sister. She is much darker and has kinky hair."

"Does your sister ever leave the house?"

"This is a terrible story. I never talk about it. When we were small children, I once, accidentally, pushed her into the bonfire of Sao Joao. My parents thought I did it because I was jealous of her. You see, my father showed more affection to her than to me. She burned her face and became blind. She has terrible scars on her face. In a way, she is lucky that she cannot see herself in a mirror. I was immensely sorry for what I had done and vowed to myself that I would take care of her as long as she lived. My father died young. My mother could not provide well for us, but I was able to get a scholarship for the teachers' college."

"That's how you became a Professora?"

"Yes, I was young and pretty when I graduated. I could have married at that time, but I could accept none of the offers for marriage because I had to support my mother and sister. Since Mother died, I live completely for Lucia's well-being. Imagine, the name of the poor creature is Lucia, the light."

"And the deep wish for a child is the reason you quasi-adopted Sezinho?"

Not quasi, Donna Anna Maria. The adoption papers are nearly complete. My sister and I will not live eternally, and I want to send him to college and have him inherit our little house."

"You are a good woman, Donna Linda."

"No, unfortunately not. I am quite aware that I am an alcoholic. I had no choice when I was young and ardent. The choice was alcohol or illicit sex. Alcohol is considered less sinful than sex."

"I always thought you had boy friends."

"No," she said sadly. "I am a virgin and I am not proud of it."

We were both quiet while I filled coffee cups for both of us.

"I guess that's why you hated the dead woman. She had in abundance what you missed so much."

"Yes, I see now that I hated her out of jealousy."

"Why don't you take your sister to a home for the blind?"

"Donna Anna Maria, I made another tragic mistake. Instead of helping her to look after herself, I indulged her in every whim. I spoiled her until she became a selfish shrew, always sorry for herself and nagging. The end was that I encouraged her to drink herself into insensitivity. When she is drunk enough, she falls asleep and leaves me alone."

"I still think that she would be better off in a home where she had company."

"I did investigate several homes. They are not very good. She would miss her drinks and her comforts. She is the cross that I have to bear for the expiation of my sins."

"You must get rid of your sense of guilt."

"My friends tell me the same thing. But I like Lucia. I would miss her and feel lonely without her."

It seemed to me that Donna Linda got a masochistic satisfaction from the naggings of her sister and had subconsciously steered her into the role of her tormentor.

During our conversation, Angela had returned without the boys and done the work in the bar without disturbing us in our corner.

Donna Linda got up at last to leave but stopped herself to tell me, "Sezinho wants me to tell you that he is not a thief."

"I know that. It was Enrico who took the candy." Then I turned to Angela. "Why didn't Enrico come back with you?"

"He's playing with Walther. They gave him something to eat. He is afraid you will beat him. He knows that you have found out."

"Ach, Donna Linda, this bar is not the right milieu for our children. Do you think we should sell it?"

Donna Linda sat down again. "Of course, you must sell it. You do nothing but worry about the children all day long, and you are not made to do such hard work. You made a mistake when you bought the place."

"Do you know anybody who might buy it?"

"Not right now. But I will look around. Now, tell me about the missing candy."

I told her the whole story and my reaction to it.

"For God's sake, don't overreact so terribly," she said when I was through with it. "Most children go through such a crisis. He did not take it to satisfy himself, but in order to acquire friends."

While we talked, Donna Anna, Senhor Ernesto's wife, came in with a plate full of cake. "I am so sorry that you didn't come yesterday, Donna Anna Maria. Here are some leftovers."

"My children said that it was such a wonderful party," I said untruthfully.

"Yes, it was wonderful. Nossa Senhora has at last heard our prayers. João sat and talked with Rosa all evening."

"That's wonderful. Never give up hope."

"Rosa is such a wonderful girl. Just what we have prayed for as a daughter-in-law."

"Do you think we will live long enough to see grandchildren?"

"*Devagar, devagar,*" slow, slow, said the Professora. "It is only a beginning. Don't stop praying."

"Yes, I know. I lit a candle for the Holy Virgin this morning."

"Donna Anna," I changed the subject. "We are going to have a fiesta tonight in our block. I hope that you and your family are coming, and, of course, you, Donna Linda, are also invited."

"Is Rosa coming?"

"I guess so. She is invited."

"Senhor Ernesto and I are tired from yesterday. But I will see to it that João will be there."

"Donna Maria invited me already. I hope I can come after Lucia is asleep."

Both ladies had left when Captain Alfredo returned from Roberta's room.

"I would like to ask you a question. But I don't want your daughter to hear. Could you send her away?"

"Angela, please go once more to Toninho's house and tell Enrico that I am not going to beat him up."

When Angela was gone I was definitely worried about what he had to say that Angela could not hear.

"How do you explain that she had a drawer full of condoms and was pregnant?"

I sighed deeply with relief. "It was really not necessary to send Angela away for this. First of all, it happens that condoms burst, especially our Brazilian brand. But she probably wanted to get pregnant."

"Why would a prostitute want to get pregnant?"

"Roberta's dream was a conventional marriage, and to give up her seedy work."

"Could it be that the man whose child she carried was the murderer?"

"It is a possibility but not a probability."

"Do you know that we found the fingerprints of the old man with the fat son on the door."

"I wondered when you called him for questioning."

"Could he be the grandfather of the baby?"

"Don't ask me. I don't want to accuse anybody. I'll help you only with the facts that would clear one of the suspects."

"But I have to follow the clue. Who of your customers is an eligible bachelor?"

"How do I know all the people she slept with?"

"Forget whether she slept with them or not; that's our business. Just tell me who of your customers was unmarried and a desirable match."

He took out a clean sheet of paper from his briefcase, and wrote the heading "desirable bachelors" on it.

"You should know them all by now. There is Chico and Emilio, but I don't think they were interested in girls."

"We found fingerprints of both."

"Emilio had the role of the male in their relationship."

"Then Chico could have shot her in a fit of jealousy?"

I didn't elaborate, and he continued, "Who else?"

"Danny is young, handsome, and has a rich father." I was still mad at Danny for his flirt with Angela, but I knew damn well that he was not the murderer. If the murder was connected with Danny, it would have been Senhor Abraham who had no alibi for the time of the murder except that he slept at home.

"We can eliminate him. His prints were not in the room, only his father's."

"Aha, then Senhor Abraham was afraid that Danny was in danger from the girl. I don't think he slept with her. His marriage seems to be satisfying enough."

"Have you found the murder weapon?" I tried to divert him because I knew that the next on the list must be Jussuf, and I did not want to discuss him.

"No, we didn't find the weapon, but it is immaterial because we know that the fatal shot was fired from the gun that was in the bar during the morning."

"Another bachelor was Joao, the son of the landlord. He is rich. But he is not interested in girls."

"That's where you are wrong. His and his father's prints were in the room."

"Pusha vida," I said. I didn't know what to say at first, but then I remembered. "Do you know that in the old country fathers often take their sons to whorehouses to give them a lesson in sex?"

"Hm," said the captain. "Isn't this a little farfetched?"

"Maybe—maybe not. Anyway, Senhor Ernesto is too eager for a grandchild. He wouldn't mind if the mother was a prostitute."

"What do you think about the Arab?"

"Jussuf is our friend. If you think that he is an eligible bachelor, you are right. But he is an upright young man and a good son. His parents live in Lebanon, and he sends them a check every month. Besides, he is engaged to get married."

"He told me himself that he has broken the engagement. He has also moved from this neighborhood. He had the gun first, and he doesn't have an alibi. Do you know his new address?"

"No," I lied. "I think it is somewhere in Santa Anna."

"Do you expect him tonight at your fiesta?"

"I hope he will come."

"Please ask him for his address. He has given us a wrong address when we interrogated him."

"You will find his address as soon as he registers his new address."

"Don't be so flippant. I always thought of you as a helper in the cause of justice."

"Alright, Captain Alfredo. I'll try to find out for you." But I was determined not to help the police, but Jussuf.

I wondered why we had not been disturbed by customers. Then I saw the cordon of policemen guarding both entrances to the bar.

"Again you ruin my business. Leave me alone. I don't feel well."

"I am sorry, but your customers will be back after I am gone."

"I think I am coming down with a fever," I said.

"I hope it is nothing serious and you get well soon. I'll leave now to find the new addresses of Emilio and Jussuf."

As soon as he left, a swarm of patrons came in.

"Do you know that Roberta was pregnant when she was shot?" I greeted them.

I saw a glimmer of relief on some of the faces. They realized that this fact would keep the investigation off their backs.

Angela returned, but no Enrico. Then Willy showed up much earlier than usual.

"Hello," he said. "They sent us home earlier because of St. John."

"How was your trip?"

"Great. They have done a tremendous job. Soon we will have enough electricity in São Paulo. How are things on the home front?"

"I caught a cold yesterday in the rain. I am afraid I have a bad bronchitis."

"Why didn't you take an umbrella?"

"Why should I? It scarcely rains in winter. Did you?"

"Why should I?" he answered. "It scarcely rains in winter. That's why I didn't take one."

"Can I have no peace at home. First thing I get home, you start a fight."

"Who started?"

"Go home if you are sick, and let me in peace."

"They told me you had a number of offers for the bar but didn't accept them."

"So, that's what's bugging you. I can't give away the bar on a silver platter. Do you really want to lose all our work and investment?"

I could have continued to fight, but I was dizzy and could hardly breathe. Besides, I had still the difficult confrontation with Enrico in front of me. I left without a word and went home.

I went to bed right away. Willy followed soon afterwards to change, but we did not talk to each other. Angela came home soon after Willy was back in the bar and brewed hot tea for me.

Finally, Enrico opened the bedroom door cautiously. When he saw that I was awake, he said, "Please don't beat me up."

"I can't beat you up from my bed. But honestly, don't you think that you deserve worse than a spanking?"

Enrico looked at his feet but did not say a word.

"Don't you know it is a sin to steal?"

He did not look up but said, "Don't beat me."

I racked my brain for something constructive to say to him to bring him out of his shell. Finally, I lifted my hand to pet him.

He backed away, frightened, and shouted again, "Don't beat me!" Then he ran out of the room.

I dozed with nightmares of police chasing me, and with deep feelings of guilt, but gradually the nightmares ceased.

Wolfi and Willy came home at seven. They had called it a day and had closed the bar. I got up for supper.

Afterwards, the children installed me in an armchair with blankets and pillows and a footstool in the street so that I could be present at the fiesta.

Then they built the pyre for the bonfire. Donna Linda had sent with Sezinho a portable record player, and they started dancing. I climbed out of my blankets to dance with Willy because I wanted to make peace with him, but after a few steps I sank exhausted back in my chair and had to send Angela back to the house for my medication. I had a terrible fit of coughing, but I did not go back to bed.

It was a clear night, cool, but not cold. The waxing moon lay on its back, stretching its two feet upward. The stars twinkled, and from time to time, a balloon floated silently above our heads.

Behind each balloon ran a crowd of children to catch it when it fell back to earth.

Although I had decided to stop drinking, I took the strong, hot toddy that Donna Maria offered me. More and more guests arrived. They sat on the low stone wall of Donna Maria's garden or on chairs. All of Enrico's friends and former enemies were present, even Nelson.

Our party was less fancy than Senhor Abraham's. We didn't have churasco, but enough cold treats for everyone. Instead of fireworks, the children popped noisy firecrackers.

From time to time, one of the young couples jumped together over the fire. I saw Wolfi with a girl I did not know, and he did not introduce her to me. Angela jumped with Danny over the fire, and at last, when the fire was already low, João took Rosa by the hand and jumped with her.

When the fire was on the verge of dying, Willy went to our yard and brought out some discarded furniture to burn. Then Enrico went and brought the packing crates and candy wrappers from under the house and threw them into the flames.

People came and went. Donna Irma sat down on a chair beside me and said she wanted my advice on an important decision.

"What is it?" I asked.

"Donna Anna Maria," she began. "I have done a lot of thinking during the last days. You know, I suspected Nair was going to the murdered girl. I could have killed her myself. I hated her so. But I did not have a weapon. That can't continue. Nair and I have made peace. We have to face the fact that we can't have children. We want to adopt Roberta's little girl. What do you know about her?"

"That's great. As far as I know, the child has no relatives other than her mother. If nobody adopts her, she will be sent to an orphanage. According to the picture I saw, she is a very pretty girl."

"That sounds fine."

"But do you realize that she is partly negro?"

"That doesn't make any difference. Nair has probably some negro ancestors. Most Brazilians are mixed."

It is strange how race-conscious we Europeans are. I always admired the Brazilians for their tolerance.

Donna Irma left me to stand beside her husband. I heard her say, "Donna Anna Maria thinks it is a good idea."

Then both of them jumped happily over the fire. Jussuf sat down on Donna Irma's chair.

"Donna Anna Maria, I don't know what to do. The police think that I have shot Roberta."

"But you know that you are innocent. That's the main thing. Even in Brazil you will have a fair trial and the possibility to defend yourself."

"I haven't registered at my new place yet because I am afraid they will arrest me."

"You cannot do that. You make a case against yourself if you are a fugitive from justice. You better register tomorrow."

"Jussuf," I continued after a while. "The captain questioned me about you this afternoon. I told only good things about you." I smiled at him.

Jussuf put his hand under the blanket on my knee. It felt good there. But then he moved his hand upwards along my legs.

"Don't do that, I don't like it," I said quietly. Jussuf withdrew his hand and left me.

The moon was setting already when a large balloon came floating low above our heads. All the children from our party, as well as a group of children that had followed the balloon, climbed over the wall of Senhor Ernesto's orchard between the bar and our house where the balloon landed.

Suddenly we heard shouting, "The gun, the gun!"

The children returned with the remnants of the balloon, and Nelson waved the pistol in his hand.

"I have found it. Finders keepers. It is mine."

"No," said Willy, "you cannot keep the gun. It is probably the murder weapon. We have to give it to the police."

"But I want to keep the gun."

"That is impossible. But I will give you fifty cruzeiros for it."

Nelson reluctantly gave up the weapon.

"Where did you find it?"

"It was next to the wall of your bar, you know, near the room where you keep the beer. It was half-covered with earth."

"Wrap the gun in a piece of cloth. Maybe there are some finger-prints," I advised.

"All they will find are Nelson's prints, said Willy. "But you, Wolfi, go to the orchard and mark the place where the gun was found for the police."

Nelson clutched his money. "Next week I can also go to the movies," he boasted.

"Didn't you go last Sunday?" I asked him.

"No, I didn't have the money."

"Nelson," I called him. "Sit down here beside me and be quiet that the others don't hear. Did you see the dead girl in the street?"

He nodded and blushed.

"Why did you not call the police?"

He did not answer.

"Did you take the candy and the crayons?"

He did not answer, but ran away. That was the end of our fiesta.

Sunday market crowd.

Chapter Seven

FRIDAY, JUNE 25

I was feverish when I woke up and I felt poorly.

I woke up Willy and moaned, "I'm sick. I cannot go to the bar."

"What do you want from me? I have to go to work," he said crossly.

"I hate to leave the children all day alone in the bar."

"Then sit in a chair, and let them do the work as you did yesterday."

"No, this is more serious. I want to stay in bed."

"You always manage to get sick at the wrong time," he said angrily.

I left the bed and steadied myself on the wall while I went to the bathroom.

"You win," Willy resigned himself. "I'll call in sick and stay in the bar. Take it easy."

He woke up Wolfi so that he could take care of the bar while he went to the pharmacy to call the office. I pulled the blanket over my ears and fell asleep again.

Angela got up at eight and brought me breakfast in bed, but I got up and had it with the children in the kitchen.

"Angela," I asked, "do you remember where we left the gun yesterday?"

"Oh my God!" she exclaimed, "we must have left it outside."

"Darn it. Then it got wet from the dew, and all the fingerprints are gone."

"Don't worry about fingerprints, Mama. The rain on Wednesday has washed them off anyway. Nelson's dirty fingers are all that's left on the gun."

"Go out, please, and get it, and get me also the slip with Jussuf's address from the money drawer in the bar. I am afraid I will have to give it to Captain Alfredo."

"Mama, you cannot do this. Jussuf is our friend."

"Angela, what can I do? If I don't they would call it an obstruction of justice, and I would be in trouble. If Jussuf is innocent, he will be able to prove it."

Angela came back soon with the paper and the gun.

"Be careful, there might be another bullet in it."

I wondered whether I should call the local doctor for a house-call or whether I should go to the clinic downtown where I could get inhalation therapy.

I told Angela that I would see the doctor in the cidade.

"Mama, you are too sick to go on your own. Let me go with you," pleaded Angela.

"No," I told her firmly. "I can manage on my own, and I want somebody to look after the boys here at home."

Reluctantly she agreed. I dressed slowly, put the gun in my purse and went to the bar.

Willy was surprised to see me. But after I explained why I wanted to go downtown, he understood.

I nearly collapsed in the pharmacy while waiting my turn for the telephone, but the girl who answered the phone at the clinic was sympathetic and told me to come right away.

From the pharmacy I went to the local police station to give them the gun. The officer in charge wrote a statement that a child found the gun near the south wall of our bar and that there is reason to believe that it is the weapon with which a woman was killed last Sunday afternoon in the Rua Bonita. I told him that I had wrapped the gun but that any fingerprints were washed away during the rain on Wednesday.

The officer asked me whether I knew who was in charge of the murder investigation and I gave him the name of Captain Alfredo. He told me he would notify homicide about the finding of the weapon.

I took a taxi to the clinic. The doctor gave me antibiotics and inhalation therapy which made me feel a lot better. He also told me to stay in bed until Monday afternoon and see him Monday at three o'clock.

I was glad about the three days of rest, but I also knew that Willy would not like to stay home from work on Monday also.

When I arrived back in Vila Alta Vista, the bar was full of excited, gesticulating people. Mylorde's testament was the cause of all the excitement.

Mylorde said that Donna Esmeralda should inherit half of his estate. The other half should go to his daughter, Bessie. He asked the executors of his will to make another search for the girl. He himself had tried for years to locate his daughter. The only clue he had for her identification was a golden cross on a chain that he had given to the child when she was small.

If the daughter was not found within a year, the money should go to an orphanage.

"Do you remember that Mylorde wanted to change his testament?" said Senhor Carlos for all to hear.

"Sure," said Senhor Nair, "this was on Monday and his appointment with the notary was on Tuesday."

"Do you remember how upset he was about the fight between Roberta and the professora?"

"And do you remember how he ended the gambling as soon as he had won the gun?"

The voices followed each other in quick succession.

"Do you remember," I said with finality, "that Roberta wore her golden cross on Sunday morning?"

They were all stunned, but then Willy said, "But the gun was gone when he wanted to take it."

"Stupid," I said, "He had to pull wool over your eyes. He was so upset that his daughter was a prostitute he had to shoot her. But he didn't want everybody to know that he had the gun."

"You mean that the poor man thought that the prostitute was his daughter?"

"Yes, and he was so upset that his daughter was a prostitute that he had to shoot her."

"How did he know it was his daughter? Anybody could wear a golden cross."

"The girl's name was Bessie, which is a diminutive form of Roberta."

"Maybe he got the stroke from all the excitement."

The voices followed each other so rapidly that I didn't know who said what. They seemed to be excited by my far-fetched conjecture until Willy said, "Let the old man sleep in peace. He was not the type of a murderer."

"Who knows; still waters run deep." This was, of course, Senhor Abraham.

"But Donna Esmeralda says that he was at home asleep at the time of the murder."

"How does she know? She was asleep herself."

"How was Donna Esmeralda reacting to the testament?" I asked at last.

"She cried and said, 'I'll find the girl and be a mother to her. Why didn't he tell me?'"

While we were still talking, Donna Esmeralda entered, dressed from head to toe in deep black. She took a cafezinho and sat beside me.

"What do you think about the testament?"

"There is a possibility that he thought the murdered girl was his daughter."

"May God bless her poor soul. But I hope nobody thinks that he shot her."

"I don't think so."

"Nossa Senhora, he could not kill a fly. He was not a murderer."

"Donna Esmeralda, do you know that Roberta had a daughter who lives with foster parents in the interior?"

"Pusha vida! What will happen to the child?"

"Donna Irma is considering adopting her; otherwise she will go to an orphanage."

"I have an idea. I will adopt the child. Then I will have a grandchild, maybe Mylorde's grandchild."

"I would like to go with you to see the child as soon as I am well enough."

Donna Esmeralda was elated with joy to think of having a real granddaughter. I didn't want her to be disappointed later.

"Don't count on getting little Innocencia; Donna Irma wants her also."

"I will talk with Donna Irma. I need this one child because I can imagine that she is Mylorde's real grandchild. I'll help Donna Irma to adopt a new-born baby. That will be better for her."

Nobody could shake Donna Esmeralda's belief that this child whom she had never seen was her late husband's lost grandchild.

"You know, some twenty-five years ago, Mylorde was a broker. He used to tell me that he had to see customers during the weekends. I suspected at the time that he had a girl friend. What could I do? I was barren. I prayed and prayed, but the Virgin Mary must have had a reason why she did not fulfill my wish."

"Then Mylorde did not go out any more. He was very depressed and was never unfaithful again."

"Of course," I said soothingly, as to a child, "there are coincidences, and this is a small world. But it is really not very likely."

A great idea came to me. If I could convince Captain Alfredo that Mylorde was the murderer, the case would be closed and he would stop bothering us.

Suddenly Toninho appeared, laughing all over his face, and cried, "Senhor Willy, give me a large box of cigars, your very best ones. It's a girl!"

Donna Esmeralda stood up. "I have to go to see Donna Rita. Maybe I can help her. I didn't know it was her time already."

"No, you couldn't know. We called the midwife while everybody was at the notary."

"After all, the way was prepared. Was it the tenth?" asked Willy.

"Are you going to stop now?" asked Senhor Abraham.

"Who knows?" laughed Toninho.

While everybody shook Toninho's hand and embraced him, I slipped silently away because I had chest pains and was feeling very bad.

Before I left, I said to Willy, "I must see Captain Alfredo. He will show up as soon as he hears about the weapon we found yesterday. Do you think he will come to the house?"

"I'll tell him anyway. Now go home and take it easy."

"Can I help with anything before I go?"

"No, just get well soon because I must go back to work on Monday."

"That's impossible, because I have to stay in bed till Monday afternoon and then see the doctor."

"Damn it, my work is so much more important than this goddam bar."

"You are absolutely right," I agreed. "Your work is much more important than this goddam bar."

I went to bed. I could not sleep, but I couldn't read either because the letters danced before my eyes. I thought about the murder. I wished the investigation was over. My teeth chattered. I asked Angela for another blanket and hot tea.

Then I thought about the children, about Angela with all her responsibilities, about Enrico who had to steal candy in order to make friends, about the Bambino who roamed the streets, and about Wolfi who was so worldwise.

While I daydreamed Angela came in with Captain Alfredo.

"I was told you wanted to see me. I am sorry that you are sick. I hope it is nothing serious. I hope I do not disturb you."

"That's alright. Did you get the weapon?"

"They took it downtown right away. Thanks a lot. You were right, it is the murder weapon. But we did not find any fingerprints except the ones of the boy who found it."

"It could be that the murderer wiped his prints off when he tossed the weapon over the wall."

"Where did you find the gun?"

"It was right next to the wall of our store room. Wolfi has marked the place where it was found."

"I cannot understand why my men had not found it when they searched the orchard."

"I can't understand it either. It must have been there all the time."

"Whatever the reason was, we have the weapon now and we are sure that one of your customers was the murderer."

"Are you so sure of it?"

"Yes, and if you are not too tired, I would like to go once more with you over the list of suspects."

I was wide awake now. This was my chance to get him off our

backs. "Take a chair and sit down," I said.

He took a notebook out of his pocket and began:

"I think we can eliminate Willy and Wolfi. Also your cousin Francisco because he lives too far from the bar, and he went home at noon. The Japanese had no motive; we did not find any of his fingerprints. We can also rule him out. We didn't find prints of the furniture dealer, nor of the boyfriend of the mulatto girl."

"Whose prints did you find then?"

"Let's see. The owner of the shoe shop, the landlord of the girl, your landlord and his son, the disk jockey, the two men who disappeared, and the Arab."

"Any other fingerprints?"

"We disregarded the other prints because we knew that the murderer must have had access to the weapon."

"Do you suspect any of the ladies?"

"Hm, the Professora had access to the weapon, but we could not shake her alibi. The wife of the disk jockey had a motive, but she had no weapon."

I sighed with relief. At least he did not suspect a female. "Have you found Emilio and Chico?"

"Yes, they have registered at a new address. We have given them the third degree. They both admitted that they have seen the girl to prove to themselves that they . . ."

He blushed and shut up. Then he continued. "The one that was at the bar testified that he left before the game was over. Senhor Nair and Senhor Carlos corroborated his story that the weapon was still on the counter after he left."

"I am glad that you eliminate Chico, I like him."

"How do you explain the fingerprints of the old man and his son?"

"I told you before that it is a widespread practice in the old country that a father takes his son to a whorehouse to learn about the flowers and the bees."

"This is farfetched."

"Not at all. Because the old man was deeply worried about his son's lack of interest in sex."

"You have a runaway fantasy."

"Not at all. I even think that it had worked. The young man now shows an interest in the watchmaker's daughter."

"That leaves three suspects. The watchmaker is a widower. He would be a desirable husband for the murdered girl. We have to test his blood to see whether it is compatible with the blood type of the embryo."

"Where have you found Senhor Carlos' fingerprints?"

"Only on the door. This weakens the case against him."

"His prints would have to be on the door. He's her landlord. He doesn't have any sex appeal. I don't really think Roberta was after him."

The captain consulted his notebook again.

"Senhor Abraham's prints were also only on the door."

"Senhor Abraham has a very happy family life. He is a devoted father and husband. Besides he is kind of puritan. I know he was worried about his son and told Roberta to keep her hands off him, but let's face it. He is not a murderer and he says he slept all afternoon."

"What do you know about the disk jockey?"

"I know that he went to her. I know also that he could not have been the father of her baby because his great tragedy is that he cannot have children. He also would not have married her if she had gotten pregnant from him."

"I agree with you," said Captain Alfredo with finality. "We are left with one suspect who fits all items in the bill. He had the weapon and if he knew that Roberta was pregnant from him, he had a strong motive. He also does not have an alibi. His prints are in the room of the murdered girl. We have a strong case against him."

"If he intended to shoot the girl, he would not have shown off his weapon and let them gamble for it."

"We also know that he broke off his engagement. We questioned his ex-fiance. She broke off because she suspected another girl. And something else. We took a sample of Jussuf's blood. It does not rule him out as father of the embryo."

"I didn't know that, but it does not prove that he is the father."

"No, there is no positive proof of that. We can only rule out the people who could not be the father."

"It seems that you are quite sure that you have solved the mystery."

"Yes, as soon as we have his address we are going to arrest him. Did you get his address?"

"Sorry," I lied. "He didn't give it to me."

"But I asked you to find out."

"I was too sick yesterday. I am sure he will register at the new address; then you can get him."

"Yes, we will get him."

"Senhor Alfredo, I have another theory about the murder and I would like you to check it out. That's the reason I have asked you to come here. Some new evidence has come up this morning that points in a different direction. Please look into it."

"I have enough of your theories."

"You must listen to me. You know that one of the people in our bar last Sunday has died this week."

"So what?"

"You never checked whether his fingerprints were in her room?"

"He was too old anyway,"

"I don't think you would have found his prints there anyway."

"Forget about him."

"No, listen. His testament was read this morning. He left half of his fortune to a daughter whom he had lost track of, whose name was Bessie."

"What has this to do with the murder?"

"He said that he gave his daughter a golden cross on a chain. Last Sunday he saw for the first time that Roberta wore such a golden cross. He made an appointment with the notary to change his will, after the events on Sunday."

"So what?"

"The old man had a stroke before his appointment. We know that the game ended after Mylorde had won, and the gun had disappeared, but he could have taken it without anyone noticing it because they were all completely plastered. Don't you see?"

I was exhausted, but I had to convince the captain that Mylorde was the murderer. Instead, he replied sarcastically:

"Donna Anna Maria, you have a very rich imagination. Why should he have shot his long-lost daughter?"

"Don't you understand? He was such a hypocrite it would have killed him to have a whore for a daughter. Actually, it did kill him. He is dead."

"All he had to do was to change his testament if he really suspected that the whore was his daughter, and we are not even sure of this."

"Then are you not going to follow this clue?"

"No, but even if we did investigate your notion, we must arrest the Arab before he slips through our fingers."

"Then that's the end of it, and we will not see you again."

"Only at the trial. You will have to testify, of course. It was a pleasure to have met you. You were a great help."

He shook my hand and left. As soon as he was gone, I got up and dressed and stole out of the house. I went through back streets to another part of the avenida and took a taxi to the address where Jussuf lived.

Jussuf was at home, and his face lit up when he saw me.

"So, you have come after all," he said, quite excited.

"No, Jussuf, not for the reason you think," I blushed all over. "I was never unfaithful to Willy and have no intention to be unfaithful."

His face fell. "Then what do you want here?"

"Jussuf, did you register your new address?"

"Yes, you told me to do so."

"You don't have much time. The police will be here any minute to arrest you for the murder of Roberta."

"But I didn't murder her!"

"How do you know? You don't remember that you slept in the bar nor how you went home. Wolfi said that you said something of going to the boy whom you left in charge of your booth, but I didn't tell anybody about it because I wanted to protect you. You have never asked about your things; they are in our attic."

"Then you do care about me?"

I ignored his remark and continued quickly, "Did you know that she was pregnant from you?"

"That's what she told me. She wanted to marry me, the cunning bitch. She got pregnant on purpose."

"Were you not surprised when they took a blood sample from you?"

"I thought that it's part of the procedure. But I didn't murder her."

"The blood test says that you could be the father of her baby."

"But I lost the gun."

"Nobody knows who had the gun at last. It could have been you. Try to remember what you did after you woke up."

Jussuf tried hard to remember, but he drew a blank.

"Jussuf, you are in danger. I believe that you are innocent, but how can you prove it?"

"I could have done it," he admitted at last. "I hated her guts."

"Do you think you could disappear without a trace, take another name and begin a new life?"

"That would be possible," he clung to this ray of hope. "It could be done. I have a brother in Buenos Aires."

"Don't take an airplane. They could trace that. Take a bus to Porto Allegre, and from there take a tramp steamer to Uruguay or Argentina. Do you have enough money?"

"No, I had to give a security deposit on this apartment, and I have sent a check back home, yesterday."

"Here are five thousand/cruzeiros; that's all I could lay hands on. You can send the money back later."

"I don't know how to thank you, Donna Anna Maria. I'll pray for you as long as I live."

"Start a new life. Stop drinking, find new goals, and do something worthwhile with your life. You have been the playboy long enough. I have to go now. May God protect you."

We embraced and kissed for the first and last time. Then I left.

I took a taxi and was back in bed before anybody had noticed my absence.

We received a letter after a few months with a check in it for the whole amount. A note was enclosed, but all it said was, "God bless you, Donna Anna Maria." It bore an Argentine stamp but no return address. It was the last we ever heard of Jussuf.

We also never saw Captain Alfredo again. The case was closed, but the murderer had escaped.

Eucharistic Congress.

EPILOGUE

I stayed in bed all Saturday. Around noon Angela came home, overbubbling with happiness, to tell me that Willy had sold the bar to a Portuguese and his wife. Later, Willy showed up to say that he was very satisfied with the deal.

After all our debts and taxes were paid, we recovered our original investment plus a tiny profit for a year's hard work. The first thing we did was to buy a piece of land in the hills, north of São Paulo. We dreamed of a little house, but we never built our dreamhouse. On our lot grew bushes and weeds, a lemon tree, and wild berries. We ate the berries and drank the lemonade from our garden. It was the first time in our lives that we owned a piece of land on our planet.

With the rest of the money we intended to buy a refrigerator, since the only refrigerator we had was the one in the bar. I went to town to shop around as soon as I was strong enough after my illness. In the Avenida São João, I met the priest of our German Catholic parish in São Paulo. I invited him to a cup of coffee in a German pastry shop.

He told me that our parish had chartered a bus to go to the Eucharistic Congress in Rio de Janeiro. They would also provide for accomodations for the pilgrims.

"Do you think you and your family would like to participate?" he asked finally.

"That would be great. We have not had a vacation since we came to Brazil. I have to ask Willy."

I did no more looking at refrigerators but took the next bus home. Before I went downhill, I stopped in the bar of the Portuguese for a cafezinho. I asked him whether he would let us use his refrigerator to put the perishable food in during weekends. He had no objections and said that was alright with him.

The family was absolutely delighted about my plan. Looking back, the journey to Rio was the highlight of our years in Brazil. The mixture of religion, sightseeing, and togetherness was the best medicine to restore health to our damaged family life. All of the family were hilariously happy during the trip. All except me. I had a secret heartbreak.

On the third day of our stay in Rio, I went to confession to a German priest who did not know me. I stayed so long in the confessional that my knees and back hurt me as if I was suffering pains of hell. But I deserved it. I had a very grave sin to confess. The priest, at first, did not believe me that it was I who shot Roberta. I had to tell him the whole story from the beginning up to Jussuf's flight.

I started with my premonitions about Wolfi and with the gambling in the bar on that fateful Sunday morning.

When the men were completely absorbed in their game and too drunk to see anything, I slipped the gun quickly into my purse while standing behind the counter. I later asked everyone whether he knew who had the gun at the end, but nobody remembered, nobody suspected me.

Later in bed, when I thought about our life in Brazil and the misery of our present life, I felt anger welling up in my chest. The anger finally found its target in Roberta who had behaved so disgustingly during the morning. I got up and slipped silently out of the house without waking anybody. I intended to go to Roberta's place and threaten her with the gun and force her to leave Vila Alta Vista. As I went up the Rua Bonita, Roberta was walking down the hill.

I stopped her and drew the gun to threaten her. When she saw the gun, she screamed and hid her face in her hands. I was so startled about her screaming that I fired the gun. She fell down without a word. I must have hit her heart. I bent down and shook her, but she was dead. I had killed a human being.

I put the gun back into my purse and returned home, took a quick shower, woke up the Bambino and went back to the bar. When we came to the corpse, I carried the Bambino past it and told him that Roberta lay drunk in the street.

Later, when I looked at the corpse, her eyes looked accusingly at me. I was deeply sorry for what I had done. Against my feelings, I touched the dead girl, closed her eyes, so that I could explain later my fingerprints I had left when I shook her to see whether she was alive, right after the shooting.

All afternoon long, during the investigation, the weapon seemed to burn in my purse. Later, when I found out about Panthera's exit to and from the bar, I buried the gun in the loose soil right outside the hole while standing inside. It was still in my purse when Captain Alfredo's men looked for it.

I wiped the gun clear of fingerprints, but I could not bury it very deeply because of my awkward position inside the store room, and the hole was so small that I could put only one hand through it. That was why the rain could wash the earth away that covered it.

The police, of course, did not look for a weapon that was buried, but for one that was flung over the wall, when they searched the orchard for the second time.

Although I was sick when the gun was found, I made it a point to take it myself to the police because I did not want them to know that the gun was half buried when Nelson found it. I wanted them to continue in their belief that the murderer tossed the gun over the wall into the orchard. It was a tense moment, when Captain Alfredo wondered why his men had not found it earlier. But then, Captain Alfredo was not overly bright. When I agreed that it was strange that his men did not find the weapon he did not dwell any more on the subject.

I was overwhelmed with remorse when I visited Roberta's room. I was so eager to go with the captain because I somehow hoped to find a justification for my hatred of the girl, but all we found was depravity, dirt and poverty. I felt especially miserable when we saw the picture of Innocencia who was still waiting for her dead mother.

When I heard that Roberta was pregnant, I knew that I had destroyed not one, but two lives. The sleepless nights got unbearable. The asthma was probably caused by my tension.

There was the constant fear that an innocent person would be arrested and that I would have to come forth and confess to the murder, so that nobody else would have to suffer because of me.

I considered it my duty to confuse the police by first throwing suspicion on somebody and then clearing him or her. After Mylorde's death I tried to throw suspicion on him, but the captain did not follow up. When the fact of the testament came out, I thought I had concocted a plausible explanation of the murder. Actually, many of our friends thought it was a possibility that Mylorde was Roberta's father. Only the captain absolutely refused to take my red herring. He insisted that Jussuf was the culprit.

When I finally succeeded to warn Jussuf, I was relieved. I had no remorse about sending him on his way. He was in such a rut that a change of scenery could only have a good effect on his life. Maybe thinking that his alcoholism had made him an unwitting murderer would cure him.

But my conscience did not leave me in peace. So, I decided to confess the whole story.

The priest said that, after all, it was not a premeditated murder, but an accident. He said that I should not confess to the police. They had closed the case anyway and were not looking for anybody. Even if I were to be acquitted of the murder, the trial would be a terrible ordeal for my family, and I should try now to pull my family together.

As a penance, he said I should pray for the repose of Roberta's soul, have masses said for the same intention, and make sure that the little girl was well taken care of.

From then on I enjoyed the trip. That same afternoon we took the tramway up to the top of the Corcovado Mountain with the immense statue of Christ. The beautiful view lifted my heart. God, who had created a world that contained so much beauty would certainly forgive a person who was so sorry for what she had done.

When we returned to São Paulo, Donna Esmeralda had already fetched the little Innocencia. She and the little Carmen were already friends and blissfully happy together. Captain Alfredo had sent the cross, the communion dress, and Roberta's money to Innocencia's fosterparents who kept the money but returned the rest to the child.

Donna Esmeralda confided to me, "Innocencia is so pretty that it is hard to believe that she is his granddaughter, but the cross is not golden. It is a cheap imitation. That is so much in character with him that I can believe he is her grandfather."

Donna Irma adopted a newborn baby and was so busy that she neglected the housecleaning and let Nair smoke and put his feet on the table in the living room.

I do not know whether João married Rosa, nor do I know whether Toninho had any more babies. I sometimes wonder what happened to Senhor Abraham when the revolution in Brazil brought a fascist regime instead of the communist government that he expected.

We left Brazil soon after the events of this story to immigrate to the United States. We have never seen our friends of Vila Alta Vista again, nor have they written to us. That whole chapter of our lives is closed.

We concentrated on new goals, the tightening of our family bonds and the education of our children.

Appendix

LIFE IN SÃO PAULO

São Paulo lies south of the equator, near the Tropic of Capricorn. Santos, the port nearest to São Paulo, has a subtropical climate and a lush vegetation with palm trees and tropical plants. Its beaches are the playground of the *Paulistas* and are open the year round.

São Paulo is on a high plateau, some 2,400 feet above sea level. It is much cooler than Santos although there is no snow or ice. The longest days in December are shorter than our days in June, and the shortest days in June are longer than our December days. At the time of my story, the sun rose about 7 in the morning and set about five in the afternoon.

When the people in São Paulo complain about the bitter cold, it is between 40 and 50 degrees. But even on the coldest days it gets warm enough around noon to go without coats in the streets.

Only the wealthiest people had heating in their houses; the ordinary folk just had to dress warm enough and go early to bed to escape the cold.

The wet season is in summer. Nearly every day it begins to rain in the afternoon, usually during rush hour when people go home from work and when large queues had formed at the autobus terminals in the center of the city. Generally, the sky clears up before sunset, but the air has cooled off and the nights are bearable even in the hot season. None of our friends had air conditioning in the fifties. The daily rains cause much mold to which I am allergic. So I suffered a lot from asthma during our summers in Brazil.

Rain was not confined to summer, but it did not rain very often in winter.

The climate influences the folkways and holidays of Brazil. Christmas in summer has a different atmosphere than our yuletide. It is not a family affair that is celebrated at home but a time of picnics and outings. We used to eat our Christmas dinner in the garden of our friends. Instead of turkey we ate suckling pigs and the Christmas decorations in the city were multicolored lights strung between the leaves of the evergreen trees looking like ripe apples.

People in light summer dresses thronged the shopping centers at night, licking their ice cream cones. But Christmas was not one of the more important holidays of Brazil.

Only a few families had Christmas trees, mostly new immigrants from Europe who tried to retain the old traditions. Since there are few conifers in Brazil, a kind of larch tree was used as a Christmas tree.

The most important feast of the year is the Mardi Gras. At that time of the year, in early fall, it is still warm enough to celebrate outdoors, yet not too hot for outdoor dancing. Mardi Gras is the big time for Rio de Janeiro where the largest parades and the most lavish dances take place, but even the more sober inhabitants of São Paulo consider the carnival as a time of wild orgies and reckless celebrations. All work stops on Saturday before Shrove Tuesday, and nobody goes back to work before Ash Wednesday.

Many people wear fancy costumes in the streets and parade in the avenues; most of them carry lanca perfume, a kind of Eau de Cologne mixed with ether in aerosol bottles with which they spray each other. It stings when you get sprayed in the eyes, and nearly all the people wear fancy goggles to escape from it.

The Avenida São João in São Paulo is the center of the activities. The municipality pays for its carnival decorations, and loudspeakers blare carnival music from noon to midnight. In our time the music consisted of marches and sambas because the bossa nova had not yet been invented.

Every year prizes were given for the popular new hits, and many young aspiring composers and lyricists earned fame and money during the carnival.

The lyrics were funny, satirical or romantic. Even now, after nearly twenty years, I still remember some of them that lampooned the shortcomings of life in Brazil, like the one of the *Alta Functionaria,* a high government official whose day consists of coffee breaks, dental appointments, shopping sprees and about one hour of work. Another ditty was about the poor man who stepped in a puddle and got wet through a hole in his shoe, and our favorite song was about *Rio de Janeiro, Cidade que Noa Seduz,* the city that doesn't seduce anyone because during the day they have no water and during the night the light is failing. This was an allusion to the severe power shortage in a country whose population grew faster than its sources of energy.

Back to the Avenida São João during the carnival. The air was filled with the aroma of the lanca perfume and the smell of perspiring, tightly-packed humanity. The street was closed to traffic, and the traffic lanes were used by groups of *escuelas de samba.*

These samba schools were clubs whose only purpose was to put on a show during the carnival. The members worked all year long on their costumes and dances. These dances were of high quality, mixed with acrobatics; the costumes were gorgeous. A group would stop in the middle of the avenue to perform while bystanders formed a circle to watch and to clap in rhythm.

The members of the escuelas de samba were simple workers who led a wretched life during the year and for whom the carnival was the climax of life. The parades lasted from Saturday until midnight on Shrove Tuesday. Besides the festivities in the street, it was time for lavish balls and private parties, for orgies behind closed doors and excessive drinking.

With the ring of midnight on Tuesday, all activities came to a sudden end as if a fairy had waved her wand to stop the dream. The revelers dispersed quickly but had to wait for a long time in the queues for their busses home.

Some of the revelers sank exhausted down in the streets and gutters. A police patrol picked them up to sober them up in jail.

At noon on Wednesday, however, they were all freed. A large crowd used to assemble in front of the city jail when the prisoners appeared in their tattered and soiled costumes. They got a last round of applause as they walked one by one out of the jail. It was said that many people had themselves arrested on purpose in order to savor this last moment of triumph.

After the carnival began the sober time of lent. It was fall and the weather became foggy and unpleasant. Holy Week with the fall flowers, the big chrysanthemums and asters used in the decorations of the altars in the churches, reminded us more of All Souls Day than of the feast of resurrection, with the Easter lilies.

The most important holiday after the carnival was the feast of São João in June. While Christmas in the northern hemisphere coincides with the winter solstice and transforms the pagan rites of yuletide into a Christian feast, the Catholic Church uses a religious holiday to guide pagan customs into a Christian observance. The feast of St. John, which coincides with the winter solstice becomes an important feast of the Church as well as the celebration of the lengthening of the days.

São João is mostly the feast of the farmers in the interior, but it is also a feast in the suburbs of the big cities.

The main attraction of the feast is the bonfire. The noise that is necessary to drive out the bad spirits is supplied by fireworks. It is a folk festival; square dances rather than ballroom dancing are featured at the parties. Young people liked to dress up in folk costumes.

A more modern addition to the old folkways is balloons filled with hot air. The balloons are made out of tissue paper. You can buy ready-made balloons in the shops, but most children as well as adults prefer to make their own with artistic designs and of various dimensions. The hot air is supplied by kerosene-soaked rags that are tied under the balloon like gondolas. When the rags are lit, the hot air slowly fills the balloon until it is lighter than the surrounding air, and it gradually ascends into heaven. If a balloon rises, the wishes that accompany it will be fulfilled; if the balloon burns out during the launching maneuver—which happens more often than not—you will be unlucky.

The ideal situation is that the fire burns itself out and the balloon sinks gracefully back to earth after the fuel is used up. But often the balloon is caught in a wind draught and capsizes, then it falls down as a fiery torch and often causes a fire. June is therefore a month of destructive fires. But in spite of laws against the launching of balloons, the late June sky is filled with little man-made moons.

Between June and Christmas is the long time of the year when everybody works and bears the vicissitudes of life without the distraction of holidays. Even the children go to school without a break. They have a long summer vacation at Christmas time and a winter vacation in June.

EDUCATION IN BRAZIL IN THE EARLY FIFTIES
SEZINHO AND THE PROFESSORA

I met a Brazilian family last summer in Europe, and we talked about education in Brazil. They told me that schools were still a great problem and only elementary education was compulsory, but high school is now free and available to everyone who wants to go there. They also told me that the *courso de admissao*, the intermediate course between elementary school and high school, was abolished by extending elementary school.

If any Brazilian reads this book, let me state clearly that the conditions which I write about were true at the time my family was in Brazil, and the present generation will still be affected by it.

Illiteracy was the curse of the masses of Brazil and the cause of their incredible ignorance and poverty. I had the impression that the rich landowners and industrialists encouraged the lack of schools in order to be assured of a continuing cheap labor force, unaware that they forged their own doom because the poorly paid workers were not able to buy their products.

Brazil's economy is right now in a boom; however, dismal poverty still persists in the *favelas*, the slums.

Only four years of school were obligatory. The children could leave school with a certificate after fourth grade or after their twelfth birthday, whichever came first. A child of twelve could obtain his working papers and go to work for the minimum salary for minors.

There were no free kindergartens or nursery schools. Children started first grade after their seventh birthday, if they were lucky.

Many small communities in the interior had no schools, and even in the cities it was possible that a child would not be admitted because the classes were filled up or because their parents had missed the correct day for registration.

Of course, this did not apply to the wealthy, for whom a large number of kindergartens and private schools were available. We were not exactly wealthy, but we had to send Wolfi to a private high school and Angela to a convent school. Enrico went to a parish school and in addition, for a while, to the little private school of Donna Terezinha. We paid school fees for all three of them.

Enrico had trouble in school because he did not know enough Portuguese, so we sent him in the afternoons to Donna Terezinha, a former teacher who taught children in her house.

The children were supposed to do their homework with her help, under her supervision. She did not take much money and we thought she might be able to help Enrico. Later we found out that she punished unruly children by making them sit under the huge table around which the children worked. Our Enrico had a lot of fun playing with the other bad kids under the table, but he never learned anything in Donna Terezinha's school.

The children who went to high school after they had earned their elementary certificate had to take an intermediate course, called *courso de admissao* that prepared them for the admission test for high school. It usually took a year for the course, but Angela took it during her summer vacation in a garage that was used by a teacher for his private summer school. Angela passed her test, and nobody asked her where she had taken the intermediate course. Wolfi flunked the admission test for the public high school, but was admitted to a private high school.

High school was divided into two sections, the *courso gymnasial*, and afterwards, the *courso collegial*, which was college preparatory. Only very few students took the latter. Danny was one of the few.

The high school in Vila Alta Vista met in the same building that served as elementary school. The classes met from seven to eleven at night. Many students who worked at jobs during the day fell asleep during school.

Between Vila Alta Vista and Santa Anna was a beautiful modern public high school, but only very smart children or children of government employees could go there.

One single elementary public school served the inhabitants of Vila Alta Vista. It was a modest building with a large courtyard. This yard was gradually filled up with wooden shacks that served as classrooms. Anyway, the need for a playground was nonexistent as the children had no play period, physical education or recreation.

The boys went to school in the morning, the girls in the afternoon, and at night the building was used for high school. In the year that my story took place, however, even this arrangement was insufficient. The boys of the second, third and fourth grades went to school from seven-thirty to eleven, the first grade of both sexes met from eleven thirty to two, and the girls went from two-thirty to six in the afternoon. All day long children tramped through the avenida on their way to or from school.

Three and a half hours are not enough to teach or learn the curriculum that remained the same after the school day had been shortened. Children who could not afford additional schooling like Donna Terezinha's school had usually to remain in first grade for a second year. The result was that fewer children could be admitted to first grade. The number of children in first grade was nearly as high as all the other grades combined. Only a part of the children that entered first grade ever graduated from fourth grade. Most of them reached their twelfth birthday before graduation and left school to go to work.

Our friend Sezinho intended to start school as soon as he was seven years old. His father took a day off from work to register him because neither his mother nor Apparecida could read or write well enough to fill out the registration forms.

At this occasion I would like to tell a little about Sezinho's father, Senhor Miguel, who does not appear in the story because he worked at two jobs and spent all his free time sleeping. We saw him only when he left the house to go to one of his jobs. He was the only man in our neighborhood who was dark black. All the other colored people were mixed, with white or Indian features.

The reason that Senhor Miguel had to work at two jobs was that he had to support his parents who lived in a village in the interior, and he earned only the salario minimo.

When Sezinho arrived with his father at the school, they were told that this was the day for registration for the second grade; first grade was already filled up, and no more children were to be admitted.

Donna Maria was quite happy about this because she needed Sezinho as a helper at home, and he could earn a few cruzeiros through errands for the neighbors.

When Sezinho was eight years old, Donna Maria herself took him to school in the hope of finding somebody to help her with the paper work. When they came to the avenida a queue of parents and children stretched for nearly half a mile. They waited patiently for three hours, while the people moved slowly forward. At last only ten people were left when a man came out of the building to tell them the registration was closed and they should try next year.

Sezinho was desolate. He wanted so much to go to school, and next year he would be too old for first grade. His mother went with him to the bar and bought him an ice cream cone to cheer him up, but he continued to cry, and his whole little body shook.

At that point the professora entered the bar. She asked why he was crying so hard. I answered for him because Sezinho was incoherent.

When I had ended, the professora put her hand on Sezinho's shoulder. "Stop crying," she told him, "I am going to help you."

On the first day of school Donna Linda took Sezinho with her to school. He sat for three and a half hours in her third grade, then she introduced him to her friend, a first grade teacher, and told her, "This is my friend Sezinho; he wants to go to school so badly but was not admitted. Please make room for him in your class."

From then on Sezinho went first with Donna Linda to third grade and then to first grade. Just before vacation he got an excellent report card and Donna Linda talked to the principal, and he was formally registered in the first grade.

Sezinho from then on adored the professora whom he considered his fairy godmother.

NOSSA SENHORA APPARECIDA

In every Catholic Church, as well as in nearly every Catholic family in Brazil, is a reproduction of a three foot high statue of a woman, carved from ebony wood and dressed in a heavy embroidered coat.

The statue is of *Nossa Senhora Apparecida,* our lady who has appeared to us. The Virgin Mary, under the above name, is the patron saint of Brazil.

The original statue is kept in a large church in the village where it was found. The village is now known under the name of Apparecida and is a shrine that attracts pilgrims from all over Brazil.

About one hundred and fifty years ago this was a tiny sleepy village of poor people, rich *fazendas,* or plantations, and Negro slaves working on the fazendas.

One day two fishermen were sitting in a boat on the river fishing from morning to night without catching any fish. As the sun began to sink, one of them wanted to quit, but the other insisted on one last try. They lowered their nets for a last time into the river, and it became heavy with a catch.

When they had heaved the net in, to their astonishment they found a beautifully carved statue of a black woman without a head.

They, of course, made another try and sure enough, the head of the woman was in the net. A head that fitted perfectly on the neck of the statue.

The fishermen carried the statue to a house in the center of the village which served as administration building, jail and, on Sundays, as church. At the time of the story, a runaway Negro slave, who had been caught, was being kept in the jail. After all the inhabitants of the village had seen the statue, the Negro and the statue were locked up together for the night.

The shackled man prayed to the statue whom he considered the Holy Virgin Mary. His chains broke, the door opened and the man walked away.

The next morning the jail was empty and the broken chains of the slave lay on the floor. Right away the people shouted, "A Miracle!" They brought a lame man into the room and prayed with him to the Virgin Mary. The man stood up and threw his crutches away and walked out of the room.

The fame of the miraculous statue spread wide and far. Many came to pray, several were healed, or claimed to be healed. The authorities of the Catholic Church were called in to explain the miracles.

They resolved the matter by declaring the statue a likeness of the Virgin Mary and gave her the name of *Nossa Senhora Apparecida, Patrona do Brazil.* A huge, ugly church was built to house the statue, the broken chains and the crutches of that first lame man, and the village's name was changed to Apparecida.

Nobody has found out how the statue got into the river in the first place because no known culture had ever existed in the area where the statue was found. Brazilians are happy to believe that Mary appeared to them as a black woman to demonstrate that she is the mother of all mankind, regardless of their color. It encouraged them in their racial tolerance which I so admired.

AURORA, THE MAID

As I told before, labor was cheap in Brazil. I could have bought myself a washing machine, but the installments would have been higher than the wages I had to pay Aurora.

We lived in a one-family house as did most people in the suburbs of the big cities. Each house had a front garden with flowers and a yard behind the house with a cement sink, a built-in washing board, and a cold water tap.

I used to soak the washing in bleach overnight. The next morning Aurora would come, wash everything with soap and cold water, and then throw the pieces on the lawn or cement floor of the yard to warm up and bleach in the sun. While the washing was in the sun, she used to clean the house. Afterwards, she washed everything off a second time, rinsed, and we all hung the clean, fresh-smelling pieces on the washing line

Donna Aurora was a wonderful person and we considered her as a friend of the family. In spite of her poverty, she was always in good humor, fond of laughter and songs, and an accomplished story teller. We learned much from her about the life of the poor people of Brazil.

Aurora was dark of skin and hair, but she was not a negro. She was a *mestiza,* a mixture of native Indians, negroes, and whites. She was a *Nordestina,* that meant that she came from the Northeast of Brazil.

Her family lived in Ceara, a very arid part of the country. They were poor peasants living in a primtive society. It was a society in which blood feuds were rampant and superstition all-encompassing. Their life was completely controlled by good and bad spirits, mostly the latter.

Aurora told us about the windowless mud huts in which they lived with just hard dirt under their feet and the wind howling through the house during the cold season, rocking the hammocks in which they slept.

She told about hunger and thirst, about bitter cold and incredible heat and about the rags that served as their clothing. But she also told about their colorful, gay, holy days, about their ceremonies and rites, their mixture of pagan religion and christianity; how once a year a priest came to the village to marry the young couples, baptize their children, hear confession, and give them communion. Terezinha, Aurora's daughter, was already three months old when she was baptized on the marriage day of her parents.

Aurora, her husband, and the baby lived in a one-room shack with her parents-in-law. For years no rain had fallen, the earth was parched, and most of the young people in the villages left to move to the fabulous South where rain fell all year round, and the streets were paved with mosaics and full of trees.

The emigrants traveled for many days in open trucks which had been fitted with two rows of benches and a tarpaulin top. They slept in or beside the trucks during the night and cooked their scanty food on open fires. They gladly endured the hardships of their truck for a rainbow that loomed at the end of the trip.

When they finally arrived in Rio or São Paulo, room was made for them in the *favelas,* the huts built of packing crates and corrugated iron that filled the hillsides of the big cities. Only a few of them found work for the minimum salary. Many of them became peddlers or pickpockets or worked at occasional jobs for less than the salario minimo. The hunger and poverty continued far from home, and the owner of the truck that transported them claimed his money for the fare of the trip.

Aurora was luckier than most. Her husband found work as an unskilled laborer because he was less than eighteen years old when they arrived and worked for the minimum salary for minors, which was half the regular salary. When he became eighteen years old, he was allowed to continue because he was a hardworking, reliable man.

They lived in one of Senhor Abraham's houses, a tiny shack in the yard with a lean-to as a kitchen.

They still had to pay for their fare to São Paulo, as well as installments on the few items of furniture that they had to buy; they had little money left for food even when Aurora worked most of the time.

Little Terezinha ate the same meager fare as her parents: coffee with dry bread for breakfast, rice and beans for lunch, beans and rice with a fruit or some greens for dinner, and macaroni with meat sauce or a piece of chicken on Sundays. No wonder that Terezinha was thin and sickly.

Rice and beans are the staples of Brazil; even the well-to-do classes ate them twice a day, supplemented by fruits, meat, vegetables and salads. The little brown beans are rich in protein and are the life-savers of the poor because they are cheap and tasty.

It was amazing how cheerful Aurora was in spite of all their privations. She was deeply religious and believed in the justice of God and in a happy life after death that would recompense her for all the sufferings in this vale of tears. She went to church whenever she had time, not only during services but whenever she passed a church, for a silent prayer. She enjoyed the holidays and the pomp of the church and she had many pictures of the Holy Virgin and the saints to whom she prayed.

She was even kind of a free-thinker, because she believed that good people would go to heaven even if they were not members of the Catholic Church.

Aurora told me shortly before the feast of St. John that they had finally paid off their debt for the ride to São Paulo, and that she would be able to buy some fireworks for the feast. I told her that it would be wiser to buy milk for Terezinha instead of throwing her money into the air.

But she shrugged her shoulders and said: "Terezinha can get milk next week, but São João is only once a year."

TONINHO THE GREENGROCER

I have talked quite a lot about the frequency of racially mixed marriages. Willy and I were members of the wedding of Chico Almão's daughter with a tousle haired mulatto. Only one racial group in Brazil married only members of the same race: the Japanese.

I cannot tell the percentage of Japanese in Brazil, but they seemed to be ubiquitous. In general, they were better educated than the average Brazilians, and many of them held white collar jobs. But the bulk of the Japanese colony were truck farmers. They had their own cooperatives. While Brazilian farmers were unbelievably poor because of the exploitation by the middlemen, Japanese farmers were considerably wealthier.

They had a way to grow more and better vegetables and fruits than anybody else, and their stalls in the feiras were nicer arranged than the other stalls.

Our friend Toninho went each morning to the Mercado Central to buy fresh produce. Donna Rita, his wife, washed and arranged the merchandise in an attractive way, and people did not mind to pay more for their fruits and vegetables than they would pay in the feira.

Toninho mixed perfectly with the other customers in the bar. We all liked him and respected him. His little boys were well behaved and they all went, as soon as they were old enough, to a Japanese school where they learned Japanese songs and fairy tales, and later, to read and write in Japanese.

Enrico liked to go with his friend Walther to this school, and he enjoyed the stories most and liked to tell me about the Shimboshis, the little men of Japanese fairy tales.

SENHOR ERNESTO AND HIS FAMILY

I knew Senhor Ernesto as a rich landlord and a miser. Donna Anna dressed in a long old-fashioned dress with a bandanna, made up in the fashion of the Portuguese peasants.

They were young, penniless Portuguese peasants, and had no saleable skills when they came to São Paulo. Ernesto worked as an unskilled construction worker while Donna Anna sat at a street corner begging. Of course, nobody would have given alms to a young and healthy woman like Donna Anna. But she starved poor little João, and painted repulsive-looking sores on his skinny little arms and legs. She herself dressed in rags and starved herself to give herself a pitiful appearance.

It worked; people gave to her freely and she saved every penny of it together with a part of her husband's meager wages. They lived in one of Senhor Abraham's shacks.

The block where our bar was was then an empty field. The avenida was only a few blocks long. As soon as Senhor Ernesto had enough money, he bought a piece of land just outside of Vila Alta Vista. Maybe he intended to farm it, but he was able to sell it soon after with a huge profit. He invested the proceeds in another piece of land. After many transactions, he wound up with the land he owned now on which he built the houses, bars, and shops that I knew.

He lived in a roomy but cheaply furnished apartment above the furniture store and Donna Anna cooked and baked to her heart's content and stuffed her son to make up for the hungry years that he had to endure.

João grew up to be overweight and phlegmatic. He never went to school after he had finished fourth grade and helped his father with the administration of their property.

When we left Brazil, João was not yet married, but at least he had overcome his shyness to a point where he could talk to members of the other sex. Both his parents as well as Senhor Carlos would have welcomed a match between their children.

DONNA MARIA,/KRISHA, ET AL.

While I was writing my story, I had once a dream. In this dream, Donna Maria, the Ukranian girl, appeared to me and complained that I had left her out of the story.

I don't remember how I answered her in my dream, but after I woke up I remembered her and many other people that we knew that I could not include in the story because I had already more characters than necessary.

The story gives only an inkling of the real variety of fates and interesting personalities in a lower middle-class suburb of Brazil. If the United States is called a melting pot of humanity, Brazil deserves this name even more. In the United States, most ethnic groups cling together for at least the first generation, and we still have Polish, Irish, German, or Spanish-American neighborhoods in the big cities besides the ghettos of the blacks.

There were the favelas for the poor and there were the suburbs of the wealthy people with German and North American areas. But Vila Alta Vista, like most suburbs, was mixed.

The personalities in the story represent a cross-section of our customers, but we had also Armenians, Russians, Poles, Greeks, Spaniards, and Czechs among our clientele. Much as I hated the work in the bar, it was a place of fascination, and the stories of our friends were more interesting than books or movies.

Maria was an Ukrainian girl who was captured by the Germans during World War II and sent to a German ammunition factory as a slave laborer. She said that they got more beatings than bread and were often raped by their captors, but after the war, they were sent to Stuttgart where they lived in the Kaserne and could work in German factories. At that time she met Krisha, an Armenian who deserted the Russian army to give himself up to the Germans.

The fate of such deserters is well documented in *The Gulag Archipelago*. Krisha knew what was/awaiting him had he been repatriated to Russia.

But rich Armenian philanthropists came to Germany after the war to adopt Armenian prisoners to prevent them from being taken back to Russia. Krisha was one of the happy ones who got adopted. His benefactor arranged for his emigration to Brazil.

The Armenians in São Paulo helped him and Maria for the first month during which Krisha learned to repair shoes. When we knew them, Krisha had a small shoe repair shop and Maria worked as janitor in Wolfi's school. Maria knew German from infancy and Krisha had learned German while a prisoner of war.

They both were glad to meet German-speaking people and we became friends with them. We used to play blackjack every Saturday night with them and their Armenian friends until we bought the bar.

Maria and Krisha had no children. They saved all their money and later bought a shoe store in another section of Sao Paulo and moved out of our lives.

ARRIVAL

We arrived in Rio de Janeiro in the middle of the night. Most of the passengers crowded on deck to admire the impressive necklace of lights around the two bays, the silhouette of the Sugar Loaf Mountain and the Corcovado Mountain against the starry sky.

We spent one day in Rio. We admired the mosaic pavements of the wide avenidas, the elegant shops, the opulent churches, the white sands and modern high rise buildings of Copa Cabana, and the open trolley cars. What we overlooked were the favelas on the hillsides. Brazil appeared to us, on that day, as a land where the gold lay in the streets, and all you had to do was to stoop down and pick it up.

After Rio we spent one more night in the hold of our ship, then the twenty day voyage was over.

As long as we were on the ship, crowded as it was, we were safe and protected as an embryo in the womb. The landing formalities of the immigration and the customs were like labor pains, and when we finally sat outside the customs shed on our trunks and bales, it was as if the umbilical cord had been cut.

We were like newborn babies who could not yet communicate with the world around them.

We felt completely forsaken, and for the first time realized the absurdity of our venture. How could sane people—together with four small children, without money, emigrate into a country where they did not know anybody and could not even understand the language.

We probably sat there only for a short while, but our fellow passengers had by then all disappeared to their destinies and we were alone in the twilight of an early night.

Agents for a transport company, scouting for clients like us, who spoke German, passed by and rescued us. They brought us to the bus station, to a restaurant, and took care of our luggage. We arrived in São Paulo in the early morning hours of the next day to start our adventure.